Prom & Prejudice

Prejudice

ELIZABETH EULBERG

Point

Library of Congress Cataloging-in-Publication Data available

ISBN 978-0-545-24077-2

10 9 8 7 6 5 4 3 2 1   11 12 13 14 15 16

Printed in the U.S.A.   23
First edition, January 2011

The text was set in Centaur MT.
The display type is Shelley Allegro Script.
Book design by Elizabeth B. Parisi

FOR MY MOTHER,

WHOSE ENTHUSIASM FOR BOOKS IS CONTAGIOUS,

AND MY FATHER,

WHO INSPIRES ME TO BE A BETTER PERSON

1.

*I*T IS A TRUTH UNIVERSALLY ACKNOWLEDGED, THAT A SINGLE girl of high standing at Longbourn Academy must be in want of a prom date.

While the same can probably be said of countless other schools across the country, prom at Longbourn isn't just a rite of passage — it's considered by many (at least those who matter) to be *the* social event for future members of high society. Longbourn girls don't go to the mall to get their dresses. No, they boast couture from designers whose names adorn their speed dial.

Just look at the glossy six-page spread dedicated to more than a century of prom history in Longbourn's recruitment brochure. Or the yearly coverage in the *New York Times* Sunday Style section . . . or *Vanity Fair* . . . or *Vogue*. Fashion reporters and photographers flock to the Connecticut campus to scope out the fashion, the excess, the glamour of it all. It is Fashion Week for the silver spoon set.

The tradition started in 1895, the first year Longbourn opened its doors. Originally set up as a finishing school for proper ladies, the founders realized they needed to have an event to usher their students into the elite world. And while girls nowadays don't really need to be formally "welcomed" into society, nobody wants to give up a weekend-long excuse to dress up and attempt to outshine one another. Friday night is the reception where the couples (consisting of Longbourn girls and, for the most part, boys from the neighboring Pemberley Academy) are introduced. Saturday night is the main event and Sunday afternoon is a brunch where reporters interview the students about the previous evening.

Students become fixated on prom from the day they get accepted. To not attend, or have the proper date, would be a scandal from which a young girl would never be able to recover.

Imagine the chaos that erupted a few years ago, when a scholarship student not only snagged the most sought-after boy at Pemberley, but showed up in a dress from Macy's (the horror!) and caught the eye of the *New York Times* reporter, who ended up putting her, and her story, on the cover of the Style section.

Up to that point, most students tolerated the two scholarship students in each class. But this was too much.

The following year, hazing began. Most scholarship students couldn't last more than two years. The program only continued because the board of trustees was adamant about diversifying the student body (and by diversify, they meant having students whose parents didn't earn seven-figure yearly bonuses). Plus, the scholarship students, often called "charity cases," helped boost the academic record and music program.

Given the opportunities, education-wise, the scholarship students try to put up with the behavior. After all, this kind of experience couldn't have happened at home. So there was a price to pay for the best teachers, resources, and connections. That price — condescension, taunts, pranks — got old pretty quickly.

It's not easy, though. It only took the new scholarship girl in the junior class two days before she broke down in tears. Fortunately, she was alone in her room and nobody saw her. But it happened.

I should know. Because that was my room, and my tears.

I was a scholarship student. A charity case.

One of *them*.

There was a giant target on my back.

And I had to do everything possible to avoid getting hit.

2.

THE STOMACH PAINS ALWAYS STARTED ONCE THE TRAIN pulled out of Grand Central Station in Manhattan. When I first took the trip, I had butterflies in my stomach, but now I knew better. Now the butterflies had turned to vipers.

Part of me should've been impressed that I'd been able to survive my first semester at Longbourn. I knew I would have difficulties coming in as a junior, but nothing could've prepared me for the cold, wet greeting given to me by several girls on my floor. They thought a proper hello was throwing a milk shake in my face on my way to orientation. I could still feel the cold shock of the strawberry slush hitting my face. I ended up being late to orientation, and when the headmistress asked me for my excuse, I told her I'd gotten lost. I heard snickering throughout the room and wondered how many people had been in on the hazing.

Most of the other things they did to me were subtler: replacing my shampoo with hair removal lotion (luckily, I could smell it before it caused any real damage), tampering with my razor so I got a nasty cut on my leg, putting crushed-up laxatives in my lemonade mix. . . .

I closed my eyes and tried to block out my first *week* at school. I truly had every intention of coming back from winter break with a positive attitude. I already knew whom to avoid (pretty much everybody except for my roommate, Jane, and the other "charity case" in our class, Charlotte). I was doing well in my classes. I already established myself as the top pianist on campus (which was really important since I was on a music scholarship). And I had a job that I liked because I was able to interact with somewhat normal people (aka "townies"). Oh, and I needed the money. It always seemed to come back to money.

And then there was Ella Gardiner, my piano teacher. She was one of the most prestigious piano instructors in the country, she was on the board of directors at countless music institutions, *and* she had the reputation of getting her students into the top music programs upon graduation. She was the reason I came to Longbourn, and she was why I had subjected myself to what came along with being a scholarship student.

I grasped on to the scrapbook my friends back home had made me for Christmas. I flipped through the pages of photos, notes, memories from my former life. The life in which I had a tight circle of friends, one that never made me question whether I belonged. I smiled as I looked at the pages filled with photos from the many traditions we started in grade school: Anna's Valentine's Day parties (no boys allowed), our Halloween re-creations of *Grease* in my living room, holiday gatherings. Then I came to the final section of the scrapbook — the pages filled with the programs of my various recitals and concerts over the years and photos of my friends gathered around me to celebrate. The very last page had a program from a concert by Claudia Reynolds, the classical pianist that I looked up to, along with a note signed by everybody: *To the next Claudia Reynolds, we miss you, but know you're going to accomplish great things. Don't forget us when you're playing Carnegie Hall.*

My eyes began to sting with tears. I could never forget my friends, but I had almost forgotten what it was like to have a supportive group of people cheering me on. I closed my eyes and tried to hold on to the memory tightly so it wouldn't slip away.

It was amazing how two weeks away from campus could give you a false sense of security. As the train pulled into the station, I envisioned a force field, like an emotional shield, enveloping my body.

I was smarter, wiser. And I knew better than to let any childish taunts get the best of me. My barrier was up and there was no way I was going to let anybody in.

There was only one person I couldn't wait to see when I got on campus.

"Lizzie!" Jane greeted me as I walked into our room. I'd visited Jane a few times in Manhattan over the break, since I lived right across the Hudson River, in Hoboken, New Jersey. Jane even came to a party one of my friends had back home, and impressed even my most critical friends with her kindheartedness. I knew that someone, somewhere had to be looking out for me to have Jane as my roommate.

After we caught up, Jane wanted to get down to business. "So, we have a very important decision to make." She went over to her closet and pulled out three cocktail dresses. "Which one should I wear tonight?"

My stomach dropped. Longbourn was hosting an upperclassman reception with Pemberley Academy. The official reason was to welcome the returning students who spent last semester abroad. But I had a feeling it was the start of hunting season (the catch being a prom date).

"You promised me you would go!" Jane reminded me.

"I know, I know." I tried to sound optimistic. But unfortunately, Jane could always see through me.

"Here, try this on." Jane handed me a beautiful black dress. I always had to borrow clothes from her anytime we had a formal event. And we had a lot of formal events.

I was standing in our room, half naked, when Jane's younger sister, Lydia, burst through the door. She didn't believe in knocking . . . or doing anything considerate.

After I zipped up the dress, Lydia flounced on my bed and declared, "Is *that* what you're going to wear?"

"Lydia," Jane scolded, "I think Lizzie looks fabulous."

I smiled. "You have to think that, Jane — it's your dress."

"Oh, right." Lydia's face fell. "Sorry, Lizzie. It's just that Jane can lend you all her clothes, but *you* can't necessarily make them fit."

"Lydia!" Jane threw a notebook at her sister. "You need to be more polite, especially . . ."

Jane let her thought trail off. But both Lydia and I knew what she meant.

Jane and Lydia's father had been laid off over Christmas when his company had merged with another investment bank. Not that it mattered much — he got a huge payout and money didn't seem like an issue. Although as word spread throughout campus, you would've thought Jane and Lydia came back from the holidays with leprosy.

As Jane and I finished getting ready, Lydia began whining. "No fair. Why can't I come? You better at least let me go prom-dress shopping with you."

Jane blushed. "Slow down — nobody's been asked to anything."

"Yet," Lydia countered.

"The reception tonight is just an opportunity for us to catch up after the holidays."

"Yeah, especially with a certain *someone* returning from London!" Lydia jumped up on my bed, acting years younger than the freshman student she was, and put her hand up to her heart. *"Oh, Charles Bingley, how I missed you so!"* She dropped onto the bed with an exaggerated sigh.

"That's it!" Jane started shooing Lydia out the door. "Out! We need to finish getting ready." She started nervously adjusting her bracelet.

Charles Bingley had spent the previous semester studying abroad in London. Before he left, Jane and Charles had started to get close. From what Jane told me, nothing really happened, since they knew there was about to be an ocean between them. Jane generally kept her feelings close to the vest, but with Charles's imminent arrival, she had become openly giddy. Especially once her sister was out of the room.

"Oh, Charles Bingley, how I missed you so!" Jane called out, laughing. But then she clearly felt that was too much. She examined herself in the mirror and added, "I guess there is no reason for me to get my hopes up. He probably e-mailed with a lot of girls last semester."

One of the most wonderful things about Jane, besides her kindness, was that she had absolutely no idea how beautiful she was. She was completely void of vanity.

"I'm just excited to see him again," she went on. "I'm sure he'll have tons of girls fighting over him for prom."

"You're being ridiculous, Jane! Seriously! If Charles Bingley is even half the guy you say he is, he'd be a raving lunatic to not ask you to prom."

Jane had promised me that Charles was different from the other Pemberley boys I'd met. Talking to them was like being placed into conversational purgatory, with no hope of being released without significant damage to one's self-esteem. The first time I met a Pemberley guy, the first words out of his mouth were "Which mutual funds do you invest in?" When I told another Pemberley boy that I played the piano, he responded, "Is there money in that?" Another had mentioned that his father was in the Forbes 400 ("and not in the bottom two hundred, either") within a minute of meeting me. A fourth had kept his eyes on my chest the whole time we spoke. And then he moved on to the next girl's chest. For Jane's sake, I prayed she was right about Charles being unlike those guys.

Jane smiled and took me by the elbow. "You are too kind, Lizzie. Just promise me that you'll try to enjoy yourself tonight. You'll have fun. I promise."

I desperately wanted to believe that I could be accepted and treated like a normal person at school. But after last semester, I had no desire to be friends with most of the girls here. How could I be friends with the same people who found so much pleasure in torturing me?

No, I knew better. I would do my best to have an incident-free evening. My armor was up and I was ready.

3.

WE ENTERED FOUNDERS HALL ON CAMPUS, DECORATED with tiny, white lights that glistened off the floor-length windows and crystal chandeliers. Even after four months, I still wasn't used to the grandeur of the buildings here. My old high school consisted of cement blocks and fluorescent lighting, not rich mahogany and stained glass.

"So beautiful . . . and this is just for a reception," Jane reminded me as we took in the view. Or at least I took in the view — Jane was scanning the crowd, looking for Charles. "Can you imagine what they'll do for prom?" she asked.

I had heard so much about prom at Longbourn. But I tried to not think about it. I knew there would be no way that I would be able to go. Most of the Pemberley students couldn't bear to look at me, let alone want to ask me to anything. And the standards were so ridiculously high. The students in the room for the "reception" were more dressed up than any Hoboken High prom-goer. If this was casual, I couldn't imagine what formal would be.

Jane was approached by a girl with dirty-blond hair done up in an elaborate twist and diamonds, actual diamonds, dripping from her ears and wrist.

"Jane, dear," the girl purred, making it sound half like a greeting and half like a formality.

"Hi, Caroline, welcome back. How are you settling in?"

"*Fabulous.* I'm *so* sorry I haven't been able to catch up with you since I returned from London. Things have been *so* hectic." Caroline began to look me up and down. "And who is this?"

Jane put her arm around my shoulder. "This is Lizzie Bennet. She started last semester."

"Bennet? I'm afraid I don't know your family. Where do you vacation?"

The questions. These questions were always the start. It didn't take too long after asking questions about my family — what they did for a living, where our second house was, the status of my father's 401K — that my true identity would be revealed.

"LBI," I deadpanned.

Caroline's eyes widened. "Sorry?"

I wasn't sure if I was imagining it, but I believe I detected a slight British accent. I wasn't aware that you could pick up one of those in a few months. I'd been at Longbourn the same amount of time Caroline had been in London, and I knew I wasn't speaking with an entitled accent.

"LBI. Long Beach Island. You know, on the Jersey shore? I'm a scholarship kid, so I don't get off the continent much." I decided it would be best to get it out of the way.

"*Oh.*" Caroline crinkled her nose as if she could smell the mediocrity. "*Anyway,* Jane, lovely to see you. We *must* catch up soon." She kissed Jane good-bye and turned without giving me a second look.

"That's Charles's twin sister," Jane whispered in my ear.

"That's Caroline Bingley?" I tried to not groan. "Jane, I seriously question your taste in guys."

Jane grimaced. "Charles is nothing like her. He's really close with her and cares what she thinks . . . but Charles is . . . he's . . ." Jane became flushed. "He's right over there."

I followed Jane's gaze to two guys who'd just entered the hall. "Which one is he?"

"The one on the right."

The two guys couldn't have looked more different. The one on the right, Charles, was walking around the room, smiling and greeting people. He had the same dirty-blond hair as Caroline, but his blue eyes sparkled with positive energy. Everybody seemed happy to see him, and he, in turn, seemed genuinely excited to be there.

The other guy was harder to read. He was tall with dark hair and a look of eternal disdain etched upon his face. He might have looked handsome if he hadn't looked like he was in pain.

"Who's the guy he's with?" I asked.

Jane let her glance leave Charles for a moment. "Will Darcy."

"Is there something wrong with him?"

Jane shrugged her shoulders. "He does look a little upset. Will can sometimes be overly serious, but his brood is worse than his bite. *If* you get the chance to know him."

I had a feeling there weren't going to be many people here this evening that I would want the chance of knowing. And I was pretty sure the feeling would be mutual.

"Jane!" Charles made his way right to her. "Just the person I've been waiting to see!" He threw his arms around her and hugged her tightly.

Jane was speechless, and her long hair could not disguise her reddening face.

Charles, beaming from ear to ear, turned to me. "Hi, I don't think we've met. I'm Charles Bingley."

"Lizzie Bennet."

He shook my hand and gave me a warm smile. "Lizzie, so good to meet you. I've heard all about you from Jane. She says nothing but the nicest things."

Because Jane was a saint. She couldn't say anything bad about anybody. And believe me, I had tried to get her to.

Charles turned to his quiet friend, who had been peering around. "Darcy, come here and say hi to Jane and her friend Lizzie."

Darcy approached and gave Jane a quick kiss on the cheek. Then he turned toward me and his hazel eyes locked with mine.

"Hello," he said, shaking my hand and giving me a small, curious smile.

"Hello," I replied. I was slightly unnerved by his expression. He could have been judging me. Or he could have been making a slight overture toward acquaintance. Or he could have been plotting a way to throw me into the fountain outside.

He opened his mouth to say something else, then thought the better of it and decided to walk briskly away.

Charles laughed this off. "I don't think Darcy has recovered from the jet lag! Lizzie, it's really great to meet you, but would you mind if I take Jane away for a dance?"

Jet lag seemed to be the least likely reason for Darcy's rudeness, but Charles and Jane were so desperate to be in each other's arms on the dance floor that I could hardly prolong the conversation. As the two of them began to dance, I walked aimlessly around the cavernous hall trying to find Charlotte, my only other friend on campus. I weaved through conversations between my fellow classmates — bragging about opulent holiday gifts, swapping tales of exotic destinations — conversations I couldn't be a part of. After a few minutes, I gave up and went over to the refreshment table and began to fix myself a cup of tea.

"Looks like you just can't stay away from your work, huh?" Cat de Bourgh, daughter of an old Texas oil tycoon, said as she came up behind me. "My dad is just like that, except he runs a multibillion-dollar corporation. He doesn't consider brewing coffee a career."

Comments like this would just bounce off my shield. No, I didn't have a trust fund. In truth, I didn't really understand what a trust fund was, except that it made people act like jerks. I always found solace in the fact that I was genuinely more intelligent than the majority of my class, and that while they'd gotten in because of birthright, I'd made my way by talent alone.

After all, money can only buy you so much.

I turned around and smiled sweetly at her. "I'm guessing your daddy doesn't think saying things like 'venti half-caf, skinny latte' is too impressive, either. But if that makes you feel smart — when really, you're just asking for a decaf coffee with skim milk — who am I to judge?"

Cat picked up a discarded cup of coffee and smirked malevolently as she poured it onto my dress. "Oops," she said with a smile as she walked away.

My upper thighs began to burn from the still-hot liquid. I tried to not make any noise as I quickly grabbed napkins.

"Are you okay?" A hand was on my arm, and instinctually I pulled away.

It was Will Darcy.

"Oh, sorry," I said. "Yes, I'm wonderful. Great party . . ."

I went to the corner to try to save Jane's dress. The last thing I needed was to go to the ladies' room. The bathroom was one of the most vulnerable places on campus, an easy trap. Just another lesson from my fine education last semester.

"Here." Darcy came over and handed me a napkin soaked in seltzer water.

"Thanks." I had to try to nonchalantly put my arm up my dress to wipe off my legs.

"I agree with you on this being a wonderful party." He leaned in. "I hate these things. Charles had to drag me."

"I guess that's something he and Jane have in common — their powers of persuasion."

"And we, despite our better judgment, allow ourselves to be persuaded."

"Yeah, well, I guess the two of us have that one thing in common."

Darcy looked perplexed. "What makes you think we wouldn't have anything more in common?"

I let out a little laugh. I had forgotten that he didn't know about me . . . and my situation.

Darcy turned his attention back to the matter of the ruined dress. "Is it coming out?"

I shook my head. While the dress was black, it had a delicate chiffon layer that was becoming crusty from the coffee.

"Jane is going to hate me," I said with a sigh.

Darcy was confused. "Why would Jane hate you?"

"This is her dress. I could never own a dress as nice as this. But maybe now she'll let me stay in my room once and for all instead of trying to turn the duckling into a swan with some borrowed feathers."

"Oh." Something had begun to register on Darcy's face. The amused look had been replaced with a slow understanding of what was going on. It irritated me that he seemed to be helpful and genuinely concerned for me . . . until he found out about my deep, dark secret.

"Yeah, I'm a scholarship student."

Darcy grimaced at the word *scholarship*. It looked like the mere mention of us charity cases caused a migraine.

"I see," he replied. He gestured again to the coffee stain. "Well, good luck with that." Then he left as abruptly as he'd come.

I stood there with my hands full of dirty, coffee-soaked napkins. I shouldn't have been surprised that once he found out the truth about me he wouldn't want to be seen in my presence. I guess this was a reminder from the universe that nothing was going to be different this semester. I was who I was, and I should have considered myself lucky that there were at least a couple people who accepted me.

I headed toward the exit. I had tried to make an effort, and now my effort was done. It was best to not tempt fate any further.

"Well, hello, Elizabeth," a voice interrupted.

I stopped dead in my tracks. My evening certainly wasn't going to get any better.

"Hi, Colin," I replied.

Colin Williams was one of the few Pemberley students who would talk to me. At first I thought it was because he was a bigger person than his breeding dictated. (At least one member of his infamous family has had a seat in Congress for decades.) But soon I realized that Colin's friendliness toward me was because he was quite possibly the most boring person in the world, and few other people could tolerate being in a conversation with him. Not surprisingly, nobody thought of giving me a heads-up before I got stuck in an hour-long discussion (although, can it be a discussion if only one person was doing the talking?) with him at the beginning of the year about the benefits of private education. (There were many, and he listed them all.) By the time he was through, he was as surprised as I was that I was still standing there. Ever since, he has sought me out at any social event our two schools have had.

"How were your holidays?" he asked me now.

"Fine. And yours?"

"Fabulous — we went to our house in St. Bart's for Christmas. The weather there this time of year is most agreeable. The record low temperature is sixty-five-point-three degrees Fahrenheit, and we didn't come close to that. In fact, we were well above the average of sixty-nine-point-eight degrees Fahrenheit, which was a blessing, I tell you. A blessing." He brushed off a piece of lint from his tweed jacket. Colin not only dressed like he was thirty years older than his actual age, but he spoke like an elderly professor — both in his choice of words and the amount of time it took him to get out a sentence. "I do enjoy getting out of the cold of Connecticut, where the average temperature for December hovers around forty degrees Fahrenheit. Which is better than the January average — but still. Where did you spend Christmas?"

"Cranford."

He looked at me blankly.

"My grandmother lives in Cranford . . . New Jersey."

"How quaint."

"Yes, quaint." I looked around, hoping to spot Jane so she could save me. But she and Charles were looking very cozy in the corner.

"How are you enjoying this reception?" Colin asked.

"To be honest —"

"I think the staff did a fantastic job decorating the hall. The lights are reminiscent of the ones we had inside our main foyer at our house in Boston. I don't think you can properly decorate for the holidays without white lights. They truly are beautiful in —"

"Colin!" I interrupted. (If I didn't, I was never going to be able to leave.) "I spilled coffee on my dress and really need to get home."

"Oh, I'm so sorry to hear that. You know, the best thing for a stain is to soak it overnight in hot water. At least that's according to my former nanny, and let me tell you, she had certainly seen some stains in her day. My brothers and I never saw a mud field we didn't —"

"Colin, I've got to go." I didn't even wait for him to say goodbye. I hated being rude to him because he was always nice to me, but I was so miserable I didn't think I could handle another word from his mouth.

I was only a few yards away from the exit when I saw none other than Darcy standing there, looking at his watch. Before he could see me, I ducked behind a column, trying to figure if there was another way I could leave. As I did, I spied Charles coming over to talk with his friend, blocking any escape route I could've had.

"Darcy, isn't it great to be back?" I heard Charles say. "You have to admit this is a welcome sight, especially after four months in dreary London."

"Hardly," Darcy said drily. "I am starting to think that I should have stayed in London. Being back has been harder than I thought. I don't know why I let you drag me to this thing. The girls here are practically foaming at the mouth over prom. And here I was, under the impression that Longbourn girls had class. Silly me."

Charles laughed. "What are you talking about? You've clearly let all that English rain dampen your spirits. How could you say that about my sister . . . and Jane? And what about Jane's friend Lizzie? You should ask her to dance."

Darcy groaned. "I don't think so. Did you know she's a scholarship student?"

"So?"

There was a silent pause.

"Darcy, not every person . . ."

"Are you so naive that you would think that the first person I would want to greet with open arms on campus is a *scholarship* student? Really, Charles? I went to London to get away from —"

A flurry of girls heading to the ladies' room blocked the view of my hiding place for a second, so I took the opportunity to

25

walk away. I didn't want to hear another word. I stayed along the border of the hall until Will Darcy had left and the exit was clear. I couldn't believe that he had so much open hatred for the unrich. Silly *me* for thinking, even for that short moment while he was helping me, that he was any different from anyone else around here.

He was the same. They were all the same.

I was the only one who was different.

4.

JANE SLOWLY OPENED THE DOOR AND FOUND ME FINISHING up my unpacking. "Lizzie, where did you run off to?" she asked. "Are you all right? I was worried about you."

"I'm sorry, Jane. I got coffee on your dress. Actually, Cat de Bourgh got coffee on your dress. Or, even more accurately, Cat wanted to get coffee on me, and your dress got in the way. However you look at it, I had a really bad night."

"Don't even worry about the dress."

"If dry cleaning doesn't fix it, I'm going to pay you back for it."

Jane sat on my bed. "Truly, I don't care about the dress. I care about you. Are you okay?"

I nodded. I didn't have the energy to tell her about Darcy. Plus, I was positive Jane's evening had been the opposite of mine. Her face was glowing.

"I'll be much better once you tell me all about what happened between you and Charles," I said.

The glow turned into a blaze. "It was *amazing*! We spent the entire evening together. He wanted to hear every detail about my holidays. He didn't even shy away about what happened with my dad. And . . . he really wants us all to meet up soon."

"Us all?"

"Lizzie, I really want you to get to know Charles."

"I will admit, he seems like a good guy."

"He really is. Plus, Darcy is considered to be quite the catch. . . ."

A laugh escaped my throat. "Darcy? I know you only see the good in people, but seriously, Jane. That guy is so full of himself. Plus, I overheard him telling Charles that he basically went away to London to get away from scholarship kids."

"Oh, Lizzie, stop it!"

"I'm telling the truth."

Jane patted my knee. "I'm sure you misunderstood whatever you heard."

"How can I misunderstand 'I went away because I'm a pompous jerk who can't be in the presence of anybody who doesn't have a trust fund'?"

Jane laughed. "Well, if he said *that*."

"Okay, I might be paraphrasing a little. I promise you this — I am more than willing to go out and get to know Charles. In fact, I look forward to it. But I make no promises when it comes to Will Darcy. Unless someone can promise me that I never have to see him again."

5.

I FOUND CHARLOTTE BEHIND A STACK OF TEXTBOOKS IN our common room the following morning.

"Whatever happened to no commoner left behind?" I threw my backpack down in the seat next to her.

Charlotte looked up from her book. "I'm so sorry. I had every intention of going, but the thought of a quiet evening in my room was just too irresistible." She surveyed the books around her. "I wanted to get a jump start on the reading for this semester, because . . . well, you know . . ."

I did know. Both Charlotte and I were on permanent probation.

Charlotte was on an academic scholarship, so she couldn't get below a B average. And since I was on a music and academic scholarship, I wasn't allowed below a B-minus average. And I had to rehearse with Mrs. Gardiner every day, which was the only thing I looked forward to.

While we'd only had one concert so far, I was starting to get a reputation as one of the top music students in the school. Since Longbourn was a finishing school, it prided itself on its arts program: music, painting, dancing. Longbourn was a place where accomplished musicians could retire to Connecticut and make a luxurious salary teaching overprivileged girls. Mrs. Gardiner seemed to relish the fact that she finally had a student who wanted a challenge and could tackle difficult sonatas. But it also meant that, on top of studying, practicing, and working, there was little time left for anything else.

"Well, believe me," I assured Charlotte, "you didn't miss much." I conveyed the evening's events. "But," I concluded, "at least Jane's happy. They both seem smitten."

Charlotte smiled. "That's so great. What were people saying about prom?"

"Nobody said anything to me about prom. Of course, nobody said anything to me about anything else, either."

"Right. Well, I hope Jane gets asked to prom soon. Can you imagine anything more awful than wasting a semester on a guy and then having him not ask you to prom?"

"Charlotte, we're scholarship students. We've had way worse things happen to us. In the big scheme of things, going to prom for us is about as important as food stamps are to a Pemberley boy."

"Lizzie! Don't you want to go to prom?"

It seemed like such an easy question. But to me, it wasn't. Did I want to go to prom? Of course. I used to tear pictures of dresses out of *Seventeen*'s prom issue when I was a little girl, imagining that I was simply one gown away from a fairy-tale evening. But that wasn't going to happen here. Because in my prom fantasy, I not only had a gorgeous dress, I had the perfect guy.

I looked at Charlotte, my partner in poverty. "I wish it were that simple," I told her.

I wished a lot of things were simple. But that wasn't my reality. In real life, I was a scholarship girl who was going to be late for her barely paying job if she didn't start moving.

Sunday afternoons at the Java Junction were always busy. Students from both Pemberley and Longbourn needed a caffeinated fix to cram in the studying they should've been doing all week. I wasn't sure what to expect on the first weekend back from break. But when I arrived, I found myself walking into a madhouse of students. I quickly tied my red apron around my waist and jumped behind the counter.

"Just in time." My coworker Tara looked flustered. "I'm surrounded by your kind."

Tara Hill was a student at the local high school, and constantly teased me for being one of *them* — in this case, the *them* being the elitists in line. I assured her that if I were truly one of them, I would hardly have been on the same side of the counter as her. And that would've been a loss. Because while I didn't really like having to serve the students from my school and from Pemberley, I enjoyed hanging out with Tara and the other "normal" people I worked with.

Not that we always had time to talk. I spent the next half hour steaming lattes, icing mochas, and trying to keep up.

"Can I help you?" I asked the next customer, who had turned around to stare out the window.

When he turned back to me, I was horrified to discover it was Darcy. He seemed just as perplexed to see me.

"You work here?" he asked, making it sound like he'd just walked into his bedroom to find me changing the sheets.

I looked down at my red Java Junction apron and tugged on my visor. "No, I thought this was a costume party. Silly me! But since I'm here, I thought that somebody's got to serve the coffee. . . ."

He didn't even crack a smile. "Right. Well, I guess I'll have a large, black coffee. Although, please don't hurt yourself." The corner of his mouth turned up slightly.

"Yeah, I'm sure you'd enjoy that."

Darcy furrowed his brow and stammered a bit. "No, no, I just meant . . . after your spill last night, you probably . . . never mind."

I turned my back on him and grabbed him his coffee as quickly as possible without scalding myself.

"Here you go." I rang up his order.

He handed me a crisp twenty-dollar bill and started to walk away.

"Your change," I called after him.

He turned back around and smiled stiffly. "No, it's okay."

"*Your change,*" I said louder, and held out his money in my hand.

"Lizzie!" Tara gasped.

Darcy hesitated and then came back over and took the money from me.

"Are you crazy?" Tara said as Darcy walked out the door. "That was a seventeen-dollar tip!"

I wasn't crazy.

I didn't want to fit in with whatever stereotype Darcy had about "my kind." Despite what he may have thought, my integrity wasn't for sale.

"You're back!" Jane jumped up from her desk when I walked into our room. "Guess what."

I took off my shoes and started to rub my feet. "Does this have anything to do with Mr. Bingley?"

"Yes! He invited us both to his family's ski cottage in Vermont next weekend!" Her voice was two octaves higher than normal.

"That's great news!"

Jane sat down next to me. "So you'll go? You'll switch your work schedule and everything?"

I *had* promised Jane that I would make an effort with Charles, and I knew I couldn't back down now. "Of course I'll go. Although I have to warn you — I don't ski."

"You don't have to ski. You can drink hot cocoa while you study, plus . . . Charles did say that his family has a Steinway grand piano in their house, so you can even spend the weekend practicing."

I had to admit, that did sound like fun. "Sounds great!"

"Yay! You're going to love Charles. And honestly, Caroline and Darcy aren't as bad as you make them out to be."

I groaned. "Wait. *They're* going to be there, too?"

"Of course. I know you and Darcy got off on the wrong foot. I'm sure it's a simple misunderstanding."

I wanted to protest further, but the look on Jane's face was so hopeful, so expectant, that I just couldn't disappoint her. She had been beaming since Charles's arrival, and I didn't want to be the one to tarnish her glow.

"Okay, okay," I said, giving in.

I was doing this for Jane. Jane, who had done so much for me. Plus, I had every intention of spending the entire weekend locked in our room or chained to the piano.

I would go for Jane. I certainly wasn't going to get to know Darcy and Caroline better.

And I wasn't going to enjoy it.

6.

THE CARAVAN WAS LEAVING FOR VERMONT AT FIVE o'clock on Friday. I had to work a couple hours after class to make up for the shifts I was missing that weekend, and my replacement was late. Which meant I had to sprint the ten blocks from the Java Junction to meet up with everybody.

When I rounded the corner and saw Jane, Charles, Darcy, and Caroline waiting for me, I realized my cheeks were flushed and I was nearly out of breath.

Caroline tapped her watch impatiently and looked horrified when she saw me approach. "You *must* be joking," she said.

I stopped dead in my tracks. Despite the fact that she ignored me all week in class, I was positive my coming with them couldn't have been a surprise.

I approached them cautiously. Jane and Charles both looked happy to see me. "You're here!" Jane exclaimed. "Are you okay?"

"Yeah." I tried to control my breathing. "Tara was late for her shift, so I had to run here."

"What on earth is on your *face*?" Caroline asked disgustedly.

"What?" I started wiping my hot, sweaty face.

Darcy was studying me, the corners of his lips slightly upturned.

Jane laughed. "Oh, I think you have some chocolate. . . ."

"What?" I continued to wipe my face.

"Here." Jane took out her compact from her purse and I was astonished, and a little embarrassed, to see a line of mocha sauce on my red, blotchy cheekbone. I was a complete mess.

Jane handed me a tissue and I did my best to improve matters.

Darcy let out a little laugh — I was sure he was enjoying this moment, and I enjoyed his company even less because of it. He went over to the backseat of Charles's SUV and opened the door. "After you." He gestured with his hand. I maneuvered into the backseat and took out my calculus notebook.

Jane sat up front with Charles, while Caroline cozied up to Darcy in the middle row of seats. I was hoping I could get through my calculus assignment during the two-hour drive. And since Caroline spent the entire time whispering disparaging comments about most of the girls at Longbourn, I was pretty much left alone. Every once in a while Jane tried to bring me into the conversation and I politely answered her questions. Darcy kept glancing back at me and my notebook, as if I needed his help with my assignment. I responded by shifting my notebook so it was out of his view.

I finished as the car began to slowly twist and turn through the mountains. I couldn't help gazing in awe as we passed huge log cabins and grand winter lodges. We turned onto a private road and drove for a few more miles. The towering trees and white snow encapsulated the car, making me feel so small and insignificant — a feeling that I had gotten used to the past few months.

The Bingleys' ski "cottage" was a large, three-story birch structure with panoramic picture windows overlooking the mountains. To the left we could see the ski trails — the massive, deathly looking ski trails. There was no way I was even thinking of attempting to ski this weekend. I had embarrassed myself enough already.

After we grabbed our bags from the car, Charles gave us the grand tour of the house. There was only one room I was at all interested in: the living room that contained a beautiful Steinway grand piano. Seeing such beauty, any hesitation I had about the weekend quickly went away. Let everyone else ski — I'd have music.

Charles guided us upstairs. His room and the two guest rooms (Darcy in one, Jane and me in the other) were on the second floor, with Caroline's on the third floor near the master bedroom. Jane went downstairs with Charles while I spent way more time than was necessary unpacking. I was examining the list of homework I wanted to get done when there was a knock at the door.

"Hi." Charles stuck his head in. "I'm so glad you're here with us this weekend." His smile was very welcoming. Jane seemed to have indeed found the one nice guy in all of Pemberley. "We're getting ready to eat dinner and I was hoping you would come down and join us."

"Oh . . ." I hadn't realized how much I was dawdling. It was pretty late and I was starving.

As we headed downstairs, Charles looked up at me. "I heard that you're quite an accomplished pianist. I was hoping you could play for us tonight."

"Oh, I don't know. . . ."

We arrived in the living room where Caroline, Darcy, and Jane were sitting on the couch. Caroline had nestled herself well into

Darcy's side, while Jane seemed completely oblivious to their flirtation. I went over to the piano and started to run my fingers over the keys.

Some girls dreamed of jewelry from Tiffany or shoes from Jimmy Choo. I, on the other hand, had always dreamed of one day having a Steinway of my own. At home, we had a standard upright that was always in desperate need of tuning. When I played on that piano, it was like trying to use a ballpoint pen to paint the *Mona Lisa*. With a Steinway, it was like I had all the materials I needed. The rest was up to me. It was a challenge on an even playing field. It didn't matter if I had money or not, what mattered was talent.

"Who plays?" I asked, almost to myself.

"My mom used to take lessons," Charles said.

I let out a frustrated sigh. It killed me that such a beautiful instrument wasn't being used. It was more for decoration than for playing.

"Anyway," Charles continued, "Henry has made his famous barbecue chicken with wild rice. You must be starving."

I couldn't look away from the shining ivory keys. I just nodded.

"Who's Henry?" I asked.

"He oversees our house when we're away. And he's one of the finest cooks in the Northeast."

An older gentleman entered from the kitchen and started putting food down on the adjacent dining room table. I wasn't particularly surprised. The Bingleys' parents knew better than to leave their children unattended for the weekend, and I was somewhat grateful to have someone I could sort of relate to.

"Dinner should be just a few more minutes," Henry said before retiring back to the kitchen.

Charles tapped on the piano. "Lizzie, why don't you play something for us before we eat?" He pulled out the bench for me. "It would be nice to have some music in the house."

"Lizzie's amazing!" Jane encouraged me.

I hesitated. I was hungry to play, to do the one thing that I always felt comfortable doing. I felt alive, like I belonged, when I played. I sat down and kept running my fingers lightly over the keys. I tried out a few chords and they rang gloriously through the large room.

Before I could stop myself, I erupted into the first movement of Bartók's Piano Concerto no. 2. My fingers began flying with urgency as the music unspooled from within me. I instantly eased up from the tension of the trip, letting out all my frustration at the keys.

For nearly nine minutes, I was alone. It was just me, the Steinway, and my playing. I rocked back and forth on the bench as my fingers tried to keep up with the challenge that Bartók had laid down. In my head I could hear the accompanying strings and percussion section. At the end of the first movement, my fingers flew up the keys one last time before finishing with a flourish.

I was slightly out of breath at the end, my cheeks flushed from the adrenaline of performing, and my mind blessedly clear.

"Bravo!" Jane cheered.

"That was brilliant!" Charles's eyes were wide. He kept looking from me to the piano.

"That was loud," Caroline replied from the couch. She looked bored.

Charles came over and placed his hand on my shoulder. "Lizzie, I don't think our piano could stand to be played by anyone else after that."

Caroline got up from the couch. "Is it time for dinner, or are we going to have to listen to more pounding? I already have a headache from the drive."

Darcy laughed. "I guess Bartók's not for everybody."

"You knew that was Bartók?" I was surprised.

He shrugged. "I pay attention in music class."

"Please," Charles began to say, "it's more like —"

Darcy shot Charles a look, which made it clear that he didn't want him to continue.

Caroline sat down at the table. "Well, I guess we know that all it takes for somebody to get a scholarship at Longbourn is the ability to make a lot of noise."

Jane came up to me and whispered, "Don't listen to Caroline. She's just jealous. I don't think she likes the way Darcy is looking at you."

"What? She wants to be looked at with absolute contempt?" I whispered back.

"Lizzie!"

"I'm just saying . . ."

We sat down at the dining room table and began to dive into Henry's wonderful meal.

"Are you sure we can't convince you to go skiing with us tomorrow?" Charles asked me. "I'm sure Darcy wouldn't mind giving you some pointers."

"Of course," Darcy said, unenthused.

"Oh, thanks. But I have this thing against bodily harm."

Charles laughed. "I'm sure you'd be fine."

"I appreciate your confidence in me. Unfortunately, I'm more comfortable at a piano than in the snow."

"Well, if you are even one percent as good a skier as you are a pianist, you'd no doubt ski circles around us. But I understand.

Henry will take good care of you tomorrow. I really want you to make yourself at home here. Consider yourself family."

I ignored Caroline's snort. Charles was so genuine and had such a positive attitude, I wished more people were like him. The world, I imagined, would be a better place with more Charles Bingleys than Caroline Bingleys . . . or even Will Darcys.

7.

I WENT DOWNSTAIRS THE FOLLOWING MORNING TO FIND everybody at the kitchen table, drinking coffee and eating an amazing spread that Henry had prepared.

"Good morning," Charles greeted me. "How did you sleep?"

"Great, thanks!" I helped myself to a bagel. "Charles, is there a bookstore in town? I forgot to pick up a copy of *The Canterbury Tales* before I left and I need to work on my assignment for English. I thought I could walk into town while you guys went skiing." I walked over to the closet to grab my coat.

Darcy got up. "Don't be silly — I'll drive you."

"No, it's okay."

He ignored me and grabbed his coat.

"Don't you have skiing to do?" I asked.

"The slopes aren't going anywhere," he replied as he opened up the front door.

It was bright out from the sun glistening off the snow. We walked over to the car in silence, the only noise coming from the fresh snow crunching under our feet. Darcy went over to the passenger side and opened the door. I stopped in my tracks.

"I thought you said you were driving."

He looked perplexed. "I'm just opening the door for you."

"Oh."

I felt stupid that such a simple, chivalrous gesture could set off my defenses. I got into the car without saying another word.

We began to listen to the ski report on the radio on the short drive into town.

Darcy turned down the volume. "Today is a great day for skiing, are you sure we can't persuade you to join us? It really is fun."

"No, thanks," I said as I looked out at the snow-covered mountains. "I don't think anybody would consider a visit to the emergency room fun."

Darcy let out a small laugh. "Okay, that seems fair enough. But I can't help but wonder why you would come all this way to a ski weekend if you have no intention of skiing."

"Oh, well, that's easy. For Jane. It's the least I owe her."

Darcy quickly glanced at me. "The dress?"

"No, it's more than that. Jane is everything to me. There isn't anything I wouldn't do for her, so coming along for a weekend is the very least I could do."

Darcy was silent for a few moments. "But haven't you only known her for a semester?"

"Yes, but we've been through so much . . ." I paused. "I don't think I could have survived my first semester without her." My voice was quiet, barely a whisper. "I never realized what a luxury kindness could be."

I didn't know why I felt the need to confess that to Darcy. Maybe it was my way to talk Jane up to Charles's good friend. Or maybe I was tired of people only seeing me one way.

I turned fully toward the window as we arrived downtown, hoping Darcy wouldn't press further.

The two blocks of town were filled with chic boutiques, organic food stores, coffee shops, restaurants, and, fortunately, a small bookstore.

Darcy pulled over and we went inside.

"Over here," Darcy said, leading me to the classic literature shelf. "I needed a copy of *Twelfth Night* last year." He scanned the shelf and found *The Canterbury Tales*. "Here it is." He looked satisfied and headed to the register, where he pulled a black card out from his wallet.

"What are you doing?" I asked him.

He didn't get it. "Did you want to get something else?"

I shook my head. "No. I don't understand why you have your credit card out. You're not paying for my book."

As I began to move to the cashier line, Darcy stood frozen. I glanced back at him.

"What's your problem?" he asked.

"Excuse me?" I replied coldly.

"You seem to have a problem not only with me, but everybody else at Longbourn and Pemberley, for that matter."

My mouth dropped open. "*I'm* the one who has a problem? If I thought you were capable of having a sense of humor, I'd think you were joking."

"I'm offering to buy your book and instead of saying thank you, you insult me. Why don't you let me pay for it? It really isn't a big deal to me."

I grabbed the book out of his hand. "Oh, and it's a big deal to *me*?"

He crossed his arms. "There is really no reason to be difficult about this."

"I'm not making anything difficult. I'm buying something for class. I don't need to take a loan out to buy a paperback."

"I don't think that's what this is about."

"Oh, really?" I said. Darcy had only known me for a few days, we'd barely had a conversation, and here he thought he'd figured me out. "Well, at least I don't have to hide behind my money. I've earned everything I have."

"You don't know the first thing about me."

I tried to keep my voice down. "And you think you know about me? Tell me, Will, have you ever had a job? Have you ever had to do chores around your house — oh, I'm sorry, *mansion*?"

He looked down at the floor.

"Thought not. You know what? When I was growing up, I always wished that my family was rich. I imagined not having to save up to buy things. I dreamed that it wasn't such a struggle for my parents to pay for my music lessons. But it was. And when I came to Longbourn and was treated like dirt and met people who were more vile and self-important than I thought people could be, I was grateful that I was born middle class. That I haven't had everything handed to me. Because having to work for things makes you a better person."

Darcy clenched his jaw. "You're certainly a harsh critic. Did you maybe even try to get to know us before you began judging?"

"When?" My voice cracked unexpectedly. "When there were food stamps shoved in my mailbox? When I had to scrub off the 'Hobos not wanted' that was scribbled all over my door? When people were throwing things *in my face* during my first week? Tell me, have you ever had a milk shake thrown in your face?"

Darcy looked embarrassed. He had no idea what I'd been through. And now here he was, the King of the Elites, telling me that *I* was misjudging *them*.

I went on. "Please tell me at what point between the taunting and humiliation during my first few *months* was I supposed to get to know people better?"

"I didn't —"

"Of course you didn't. *That's* my point."

I walked up to the counter and tried to not feel self-conscious when I had to flatten my dollar bills wrinkled from the Junction tip jar in order to pay. Once the purchase was complete, I walked back to the car without even looking at Darcy. I grabbed the handle before he could open the door for me.

"In case I haven't made myself clear," I said, once he'd caught up, "I want you to know that I have absolutely no interest in you or your money." I got in the car and slammed the door shut.

We drove back in silence. I ran up to my room as soon as we got back to the cabin. I didn't relax until I heard everyone else leave for the slopes.

8.

ESPITE THE ROCKY MORNING, I ENDED UP HAVING A GREAT day at the Bingleys' ski house. I got caught up on all my homework, even managing to read ahead in a couple classes, and gave Henry a mini-concert on the Steinway.

I was on my second cup of Henry's amazing hot chocolate when everyone else returned from their afternoon on the slopes.

Caroline entered with Darcy, laughing and talking his ear off. I picked up my English anthology book and decided I could get even further in my reading.

"Hey, Lizzie, how was your day?" Charles asked the second he and Jane entered. He brushed off the snow from his jacket and helped steady Jane as she removed her boots. Their cheeks were bright red from the cold.

"It was great," I replied. "Thanks so much for having me."

"Anytime!" Charles waited until everybody else was upstairs before asking me his next question. "Um, Lizzie, would you be okay if I took Jane out to dinner tonight? I know that Caroline can be, well, not the most tolerable of people, but you'd have Darcy here to protect you."

I tried to not choke on my hot chocolate. It was clear that Charles meant every word he was saying, and at the same time had no idea what he was talking about. Despite my growing displeasure with Darcy and my extreme desire to avoid Caroline, I wanted Jane to be happy. Sometimes friends have to suffer for their friends' happiness.

"Of course, Charles," I replied. "Have fun!"

I went upstairs and helped Jane prepare for the evening. She was ecstatic to finally go on a real date with Charles.

My own dinner was even more awkward than I could have imagined. I kept to myself, only speaking to compliment Henry or offer help. Mostly I felt like I was a third wheel on a date. Caroline kept flirting with Darcy, reaching across the table to touch his hand at any chance she could get. Darcy, for his part, seemed as bored as ever, especially when Caroline brought up prom. Which she did . . . twenty-seven times (I counted).

"There are so many responsibilities being head of the prom committee," Caroline stated. (Make that twenty-eight times.)

Darcy pushed away his plate. "Do you think it would be possible to have an evening that doesn't revolve around talking about prom?"

Caroline opened her mouth, but paused. She began to twirl her hair around her finger. "You're right. . . ." She smiled sweetly at Darcy. "Let's get a nice bottle of wine and start a fire."

He shook his head. "I should get some reading done tonight."

"Ugh, reading? On a Saturday night?"

I tried to not laugh as I got up and cleared my place. "Please let me help you with the dishes, Henry," I said once I got back to the kitchen. "Don't make me go back out there." I nodded toward the dining room.

He shook his head. "My dear, you have no idea how long I've had to put up with Miss Bingley. Why do you think I don't use the dishwasher?" He gestured toward the stainless-steel industrial dishwasher to his right as he filled up the sink to manually do the dishes. He gave me a wink as I headed to the living room.

Caroline was mindlessly flipping through the channels on the large flat screen against the wall while Darcy was busy on his laptop. I curled up on the chaise longue and tried to read. As much as I enjoyed Chaucer, the Caroline Bingley Show was much more entertaining.

She leaned over to watch Darcy type. "Tell Georgiana I say hello."

"I already did — do you want me to tell her again?" Darcy didn't even look up from the screen.

Caroline placed her hand on Darcy's shoulder. "Well, I just think it is so sweet of you to check up on your sister as much as you do."

Darcy didn't respond and kept typing.

"Hmmm." Caroline yawned exaggeratedly. "What an *amazing* day on the slopes." She got up and began stretching in front of Darcy. She took a deep breath as she reached her arms up to the ceiling, a motion that exposed her midriff conveniently at Darcy's eye level. She continued stretching, bending over to the side and letting out a loud sigh.

Darcy closed his laptop, much to Caroline's delight. But then he went over to the couch beside me and picked up his book, not giving Caroline a second glance.

Caroline slouched down on the couch beside him. Darcy was entrenched in his book. "Ooh," Caroline cooed. "What a *beautiful* evening. Yes, I think it is a *perfect* evening to read." She bit her lip and went over to the bookshelf and selected a book at random.

She pretended to be interested in *Great Expectations*. But after ten minutes, her own expectations had clearly not been met, and she threw the book down.

"Lizzie," Caroline said to me. I was in such shock that she was addressing me directly I didn't respond right away. "Lizzie, do you want me to teach you some yoga moves?"

I didn't know how to react. I automatically assumed that she was setting me up for something.

Darcy set down his book and started studying me as Caroline began doing very complicated poses, obviously trying to impress him.

"Not your thing?" Darcy asked me.

I shrugged. "Yeah, I guess not."

Caroline, satisfied that she had outshined me, sat down on the floor facing us with her legs crossed. "Yoga isn't for everybody. I just *really* try to challenge myself physically, as well as *intellectually*, every day." I had to bite the inside of my cheeks to stop from laughing. "I have to admit that I'm not nearly the sibling to

Charles as you are to Georgiana." Caroline reached over and touched Darcy on his knee.

"Do you have any brothers or sisters, Lizzie?" Darcy asked.

I shook my head.

"Your parents must be sad to have you so far away." He looked genuinely interested in my family life.

Before I could answer, Caroline kept prodding on. "*I* try my best to be a good sister, but I have a tendency to take on the big-sister role with so many of my friends. It's hard sometimes, when you put *so* many others first."

Darcy kept staring at me, and it was making me uncomfortable.

"Not that *you* have any faults, Darcy," Caroline continued. I couldn't tell whether she was serious or not.

Darcy turned his attention away for a second to look at her. "Nobody's perfect."

I let out a laugh. He looked over at me. "Do you think you're perfect?" he asked.

"No, no, not at all. Far from it. I'm just interested in hearing what you think *your* faults are." I found myself enjoying the conversation.

"Well." He paused. "Everybody has them, and I'm certainly not an exception. I can sometimes have a bit of a short fuse.

I'm not the most forgiving of people. And I'm sure I would be bad at yoga." He looked at me. "Would you care to jump in?"

I tried to be polite. "I haven't known you for that long."

"But I'm sure you have something to say on the subject?" I didn't need to be asked twice.

"I guess the fact that you seem to hate everybody and everything could be considered a weakness."

"And I guess your ability to wildly misunderstand people is yours."

Caroline jumped to her feet and turned on the TV. She sat back down next to Darcy and started droning on and on about what movie to order. Neither Darcy nor I expressed any opinion, but Caroline didn't seem to notice or care.

As long as Darcy wasn't talking to me, she was happy.

9.

HE RIDE BACK TO SCHOOL THE NEXT DAY WAS UNEVENTFUL. Charles and Jane were in front laughing and enjoying themselves. Caroline continued relentlessly dropping the P-word (sixty-eight times) to Darcy, who spent the entire trip staring out the window. He ignored me the entire way home, which made me very happy.

I had switched my shift at work for the trip, so I had to work on that Sunday night. I preferred Sunday afternoons since it was always busy, so the time just flew. And we got more tips.

"What are you doing here?" I asked Tara when I arrived.

She looked exhausted. "James called in sick, so I'm doing double duty today."

"Yikes." I grabbed my apron. "Well, if it's quiet, you can probably go home early."

I started wiping down the counter and cleaning up the tables. There were only a few customers in the seating area, nobody I recognized. I practically had the orders of the Sunday afternoon regulars memorized so at least tonight would be a nice change of pace.

"Elizabeth?" I looked up to find Colin studying me.

"Oh, hey, Colin. What can I get for you?" I walked over to the counter and tried to look busy so I wouldn't be stuck in a conversation with him.

"I didn't think you worked on Sunday nights."

"I had to trade shifts."

"How nice of you. I figured there had to be a reason. You seem to be someone with a disciplined schedule, which I greatly admire. How was your weekend?"

"Good . . . yours?"

He studied the blackboard menu for a few moments. "It was very pleasant. Thank you for asking."

"No problem. Can I get you something?"

Colin placed his order after what seemed like an hour's deliberation. As I steamed the milk for his latte, I couldn't help but feel he was studying my every move. I wasn't the kind of girl that thought every guy was checking her out, but Colin's gaze seemed to linger over me.

"Here you go," I said as I handed him his order, hoping there was enough finality in my tone to end the conversation.

"Wonderful. Thank you, Elizabeth."

I smiled and began to wipe down the espresso machine, even though it was already clean. Colin eventually got the hint and left.

"Tara," said one of the few remaining customers from a nearby table, "I don't know how you deal with those Pemberley guys."

"As I recall," Tara replied, "*you* were once a Pemberley guy, Wick."

I hadn't noticed this guy before, which was surprising since he was very cute with his short, dirty-blond hair and hazel eyes.

He laughed. "Well, I *did* get kicked out. You can't really count that against me."

Tara motioned toward me. "You better be careful what you say — Lizzie here is a Longbourn girl."

He got up from his seat and approached the counter. "A Longbourn girl working at the Java Junction?"

"Make that Longbourn *scholarship* girl," I corrected.

He smiled warmly at me and extended his hand. "Longbourn scholarship girl, former Pemberley scholarship boy."

I shook his hand. "Pleased to meet you. Elizabeth Bennet, but you can call me by my commoner name: Lizzie."

"Ah, George Wickham, but my friends call me Wick. So, obviously, at Pemberley everybody called me George."

"A Pemberley scholarship boy? I thought such things were an urban legend."

He laughed. "True, true. We're a rare breed. More difficult to spot than Bigfoot or the Loch Ness Monster."

"Wick here is the rarest of rare," Tara said. "He's a townie who made it through Pemberley's gates."

"Wait a second." I looked at him suspiciously. "The esteemed Pemberley institution would let in . . . a *local*? The scandal!"

"Yes, oddly enough, it didn't rain frogs. It was the strangest thing." He had an easy laugh about him, very different from any guy I'd met here. I instantly liked him.

"I know. All the girls in my dorm are convinced I'm single-handedly bringing the apocalypse to Longbourn."

"And by apocalypse, you mean noncouture outfits?"

"Wow. You really did go to Pemberley. Only a Pemberley boy would know what 'couture' means."

He nodded his head and blushed. "You caught me. You can kick the boy out of Pemberley . . ."

"You really got kicked out?"

He grimaced. "Yeah, I guess there is only so much charity one school is able to give. . . ."

"Or scholarship students that can be tolerated."

"I see you're a quick study." He winked at me. I noticed that he had cute dimples when he smiled.

I could feel my pulse quicken. I didn't even notice when the bell signaled the front door opening. Wick looked over to see who it was. Once he did, he suddenly tensed up, his entire demeanor changing.

I turned around to see Darcy staring at us with a look of utter contempt on his face.

Wick abruptly left the counter and returned to his seat. Darcy's eyes followed him the entire time, his jaw clenched tightly. Wick picked up his book and turned away so Darcy couldn't see his face.

"Can I get you something?" I asked coldly.

Darcy jerked back to life. For an instant he looked at me as if I had somehow betrayed him. He shook his head and his stoic facade returned to his face. "Um, yes." His eyes darted back to Wick again. "I guess I'll have a large decaf, please."

There was something about the former scholarship boy that had rattled Darcy. Which made me like Wick even more.

I handed Darcy his coffee and rang him up. Before he left, he hesitated for a moment. "How late are you working tonight?" he asked.

I shrugged. "Depends. Why?"

He began to play with the lid of his drink. "Is it really safe for you to be walking back to the dorm this late at night?"

"Do you mean besides the usual torture at the hands of my fellow student body?"

Darcy clenched his jaw.

"I'll be fine."

He nodded and walked out. He stared straight ahead as he passed by Wick. As soon as the door swung shut, Wick turned to me and said, "Well, that was awkward."

"I take it you know Will Darcy from your Pemberley days?"

He sighed. "Yes, unfortunately. You could say that we were once on friendly terms. But you seem to be friends with him, so . . ."

I groaned. "Hardly. I've known him for a week, and I find him to be the most egotistical, condescending person on the planet."

Wick laughed. "So you *do* know him well."

"You got me there."

Wick approached the counter. "You really need to start being more careful about who you're seen hanging out with."

I smiled at him. "Are you referring to Darcy or yourself?"

"Depends on who you ask."

"Hmm, I guess since there isn't a way for the esteemed ladies of Longbourn to despise me even more, I will hang out with whoever I choose."

"Well, then, Longbourn scholarship girl, do you think you'd ever entertain giving charity to a disgraced Pemberley boy such as myself?"

"What do you have in mind?"

"Your phone number would be a good start."

I gave it to him without hesitation.

I was ready for a good start.

10.

WE HAD OUR FIRST DATE ON WEDNESDAY NIGHT. WICK took me to a pizza place that was in a part of town that I hadn't been to before, a very non-Longbourn establishment.

"Hey, Wick!" a girl behind the counter greeted him. "Couple of slices?"

"I didn't know you were working tonight." He leaned over the counter and gave her a kiss on the cheek. "Couple slices would be great. Lizzie, this is Cassie. Cassie, this is Lizzie." He motioned toward me and the girl smiled at me. "I'm saving her from the elitists over at Longbourn." He looked over his shoulder and then said in an exaggerated whisper, "She's a *scholarship student.*"

I couldn't help but laugh. I knew that nobody in this place would care. It was nice to be somewhere that I didn't feel the need to constantly look over my shoulder or think that I was being set up.

"Here you go." Cassie handed us each two slices. "You know your money isn't good here, Wick," she said as Wick reached into his pocket for his wallet.

"Aww, you're the best." He winked at her and we headed over to a booth. "See, Lizzie, you need to start finding the right kind of friends." He motioned down at our free food. "I've known Cassie since kindergarten. There's a group of us that have been close friends for ages. I don't remember life before them, you know? I'm sure you have people like that back home. It was hard for me to leave them behind and I was only down the road; I can't imagine what it must be like for you."

It was the first time in a while that I'd felt comfortable and open around a new person. Being with Wick felt normal, natural. He was open, honest, and self-deprecating in a very, very irresistible way.

"I still can't believe a Longbourn girl has agreed to be seen with me in public," he said after I'd told him more about life back home in Hoboken, and the switch to Longbourn. "The prima donna police have probably sent out a search party."

"Not likely. They're probably changing the locks as we speak."

"Still" — he gave me a smile that made my stomach flip — "you're a brave one."

"Believe me, the bravest thing I'll be doing this evening is entering my dorm. The goal is to try to get back to my room without someone throwing something in my face. But you're all too familiar with the treatment of our kind."

Wick played with the wrapper of his straw. "Actually, things weren't that bad for me at Pemberley."

"Really?"

For the first time since I'd met him, I didn't know whether or not to believe him. I couldn't comprehend that the guys at Pemberley would have any compassion for people like us.

"Really. I even had friends, if you can imagine that."

"Wow, that's impressive. I have Jane and Charlotte, but that's it. Jane is always trying to get me to go out more, but every time I do, the evening ends in either bodily or emotional harm. She's pretty relentless, though. I've already agreed to go to this party on Saturday night, despite my better judgment."

"Charles Bingley's party?"

I was surprised. "Yes — how did you know about that?"

"You don't give us townies enough credit. We find out about the parties, and a few of us usually crash. With all the students around, nobody seems to notice."

"Please tell me you're going to come on Saturday." I tried to hide any hint of desperation in my voice. Having Wick there would make it bearable. Plus, I wanted to spend more time with him.

"Now you've put me in a tough spot. If you're going to be there, how could I not show up?" Wick smiled at me, but then his smile faded. "Sadly, I have a feeling someone else will be there, and there's no way I'd be welcome." Wick hesitated. "There's something I want you to know, and I want you to hear it from me."

"Okay . . ." I leaned in.

"It's about why I got kicked out of Pemberley."

"Wick, you don't need to —"

"Yes, I do. I'm surprised people haven't started trying to turn you against me yet."

I hadn't really told anybody about Wick. Jane knew I'd met someone from town, but I hadn't told her he was a former Pemberley student. I didn't know why, but I wanted to keep Wick to myself.

"I don't care what anybody thinks of you," I told him now. "You should realize that I would know better than to believe anything anybody at Longbourn or Pemberley would say to me."

Wick nodded. "I'm so thankful my caffeine habit brought you into my life."

What a clear, powerful emotion — thankfulness. It hadn't occurred to me in a long time that I could be someone that another person would be thankful for. Not for anything I'd done or said, but simply for who I was, and who I had the potential to be. After spending the school year in a world of torture (at worst) and indifference (at best), to have such open thankfulness expressed to me gave me something I hadn't felt in a long time: hope. Maybe this semester was going to be good after all.

"Okay." Wick took a deep breath. "Here's the story. I started last year as a sophomore. Met a lot of cool people, and the fact that I was a scholarship student wasn't an issue. I knew a lot about the students at Pemberley from being a townie, and Darcy and his family's reputation preceded him. I was looking forward to meeting the infamous William Darcy and we hit it off really well. We were friends from the moment we met.

"Darcy took me under his wing. It was only a few weeks into the semester, and he brought me into the city to meet his family. I fell in love with them. His dad is this incredible man, which is why I don't like saying anything bad about Darcy, because his father is a kind, generous person. He even arranged for me to have a summer job last year at his law firm. That would have set me up — not only with a way to earn money, but to get experience that would have been amazing on my college transcript. Things were going well for me. And Darcy couldn't take it. He loved having me under his wing, having some sort of control over me. But he didn't like seeing me fly by myself, making things happen without his influence. He became increasingly competitive with me. And when he thought he might lose, he stabbed me in the back. Before I knew what was happening, I was being escorted off campus."

I gasped. "*Darcy* got you kicked out of Pemberley?"

Wick nodded, the color draining from his face.

"I don't believe it. How could anybody be so awful?" A knot formed in my stomach. "Why would he do that?"

"Maybe it was jealousy over my growing relationship with his father. That's all I could think of. I spent most of spring break with his family, and while he was his usual cold and distant self, I didn't understand the treachery he was capable of. I went home for a couple days before returning to campus, and in that time, he set his plan in motion. When I got to my dorm room, campus security was waiting for me."

"But that's ridiculous. They can't just kick you out for no reason."

"Oh, they had some trumped-up charges, some accusations he'd made. But what would I fight them with? My family didn't have money for an attorney. And the Darcy men had been going to Pemberley for generations. I'd been going for months."

My mind was swirling with what Wick told me. "We can't let him get away with this."

Wick leaned back in his seat. "Someday, Darcy will get what's coming to him, but it isn't going to be from me. I couldn't do that to Mr. Darcy. It's not his fault that his son is a liar and a scoundrel."

"You're a far better person than I," I said.

"Hardly. After all, I'm going to crash a party this weekend."

That was really all I wanted to hear Wick say. But my mind kept reeling over what Darcy had done. Jane had nearly convinced me that I'd been too harsh on the guy, but apparently I hadn't been harsh enough.

As Wick drove me back to campus, I didn't want the evening to end. I didn't want to have to go back to the taunts and bullying. I liked spending time with someone who was like me.

He parked the car and turned off the engine. "Do you need a moment to prepare for battle?" he asked, only half joking.

"I guess." I looked at the beautiful building that had been my home for the past five months.

"I had a really great time tonight."

"Me too."

Wick leaned over . . . and gave me a hug. "I'll see you on Saturday," he murmured.

"Promise?"

He smiled at me. "Promise."

11.

I CAME CLEAN TO JANE THE NEXT EVENING AT DINNER. IT should've been suspected that when I relayed Wick's story to her, she didn't share in my disgust at Darcy's actions.

"George Wickham, Lizzie? I haven't heard good things about him." Jane looked worried.

"There's a surprise."

"I'm sure there has to be an explanation for all of this. First, Darcy wouldn't do something like that. Second, Charles would never have a friend who was so despicable. It's probably just a simple misunderstanding."

"Misunderstanding?" I was astonished. "Why is it that I'm always misunderstanding something? How could someone misunderstand being expelled from school without just cause? Didn't you hear anything about it last year?"

Jane looked thoughtful. "I do remember he got kicked out, and that Charles knew him, but it wasn't something Charles talked to me about."

I couldn't believe that someone getting kicked out of Pemberley wouldn't be gossip du jour at Longbourn.

Jane continued. "I'll ask Charles and see what he has to say. But, Lizzie, just be careful. And please give Darcy a chance to explain his side. You have him painted as this maniacal villain, and it couldn't be further from the truth."

"You're just saying that because Darcy being a vengeful loon would reflect poorly on Charles."

Jane ignored me and cut up her salmon.

Our silence lasted only a moment, until Lydia stormed over to our table and dropped down her overflowing tray. "Jane, I just spoke with Mommy and she said she talked to Vera about your prom dress."

Jane looked around the dining hall. "Shh, Lydia. I haven't been asked to prom yet. Keep it down."

Lydia grunted. "Please, Jane. Anyway, Mommy said that you have an appointment with Vera when we go home over Presidents' Day weekend, and then you'll have your fitting over spring break. *Vera* — aren't you just dying?"

I believed Jane was dying, but from embarrassment of her brash sister. Lydia shoved several French fries in her mouth and asked, "Where are you going to get your dress, Lizzie?"

"Well, I highly doubt I'll be going to prom. I guess *if* I go, I'll probably just get it at Macy's or something."

Lydia's jaw dropped open. "You can't do that! It's *prom!*"

I took a deep, calming breath. "I know, but it's just one night and I really think it's silly to spend thousands of dollars on a dress you only wear once." I turned to Jane. "No offense."

"None taken," she replied. "Lydia, you really need to learn to be more modest. Not everybody is lucky enough to have connections with designers."

Lydia snorted. "Please! This school is all about connections. But I haven't told you everything yet. Mommy said that we can't go anywhere over spring break this year. Can you believe that? She said that since Daddy hasn't gotten a job yet, we shouldn't go galloping through Europe."

"I'm sure she said *gallivanting* through Europe, and I agree with Mom, Lydia. We're going to have to start making some . . . sacrifices." Jane looked uncomfortably at me. She knew that their sacrifices would be of the business- instead of first-class variety.

"That's so not fair!" Lydia pouted. "It isn't *our* fault that Daddy's business was sold. Why do *we* have to be punished?"

"Lydia!" Jane exclaimed. "Enough! You sound like a spoiled brat. You should feel lucky that Dad got a nice severance package or we'd be out on the street. I don't want to hear another word about this." Jane got up from the table, and I joined her. How they both came from the same family, I would never understand.

Jane put her tray on the conveyer belt. "I'm really sorry about that, Lizzie. She was always very hyper and into materialistic things, but being here has made her worse. I don't know what I'm going to do with her." She looked behind her to make sure Lydia wasn't in earshot. "I haven't told her yet about the party on Saturday. Charles told me to invite her, but . . ."

I understood. Lydia could be a little too much at times.

"You're still coming, right?" Jane asked. "It should be fun."

We'd had variations of this conversation so many times before, with Jane telling me something would be fun and it turning into a headache for me.

"Of course," I told her as I always did.

I was, after all, excited about *this* party. Just not for the reasons Jane thought. I didn't want to tell her it was because there would be some unexpected guests. I should've felt some remorse, since Charles had been nothing but kind to me. But my desire to spend more time with Wick eclipsed any feeling of betrayal I had.

12.

JANE, BEING JANE, ENDED UP INVITING LYDIA TO CHARLES'S party. It was either because she is perhaps the greatest (and most forgiving) older sister on the planet, or because she was in especially good spirits, since Charles had asked her out on a date for Sunday. That would make two nights in a row they would spend together.

Maybe Jane's mother had been right in giving her old friend Vera a call.

Nothing could ruin Jane's mood, and because I was going to be seeing Wick, nothing could ruin my mood, either. For the first time since I'd arrived at Longbourn, I was genuinely excited to be getting ready for a party.

I spent the majority of Saturday going through Jane's closet, trying to figure out what to wear. I didn't want to wear anything that screamed expensive, since I didn't want Wick to think I was like every other girl at Longbourn. But I *did* want to look nice for him.

Jane studied herself in the mirror while I debated between which earrings to wear with the jeans and gray, fitted cashmere sweater I'd borrowed.

Lydia came barging in. "My first upperclassman party! I am *so* excited. Freshman boys are, like, so childish."

Jane studied her sister with wide eyes. Lydia was wearing a very short skirt and had enough makeup on to put a circus performer to shame. Jane grabbed a tissue and started wiping Lydia's face.

"Jane, stop it!" Lydia protested.

Jane was not deterred. "Lydia, you shouldn't cover up your natural beauty."

My hand paused as I was putting on another coat of mascara. Since she hadn't been talking to me, I continued. But a little more lightly than before.

"Now, remember what we talked about." Jane sat down next to Lydia, who nodded.

Jane had only allowed Lydia to come after Lydia agreed she wouldn't talk about money or prom dresses.

"Are we ready?" Jane asked as she studied herself in the mirror one last time. I think she was asking herself more than us. She took a deep breath and opened the door.

We arrived at a large private room at one of the upscale restaurants in town that catered to the faculty, students, and parents of Longbourn and Pemberley. It was a beautiful space, filled with oversize couches, a large window overlooking the river, candles, and a slightly elevated stage where some students were already dancing.

I scanned the room for Wick, but couldn't see him anywhere.

"Who are you looking for?" Jane asked when she caught me surveying the crowd.

"Just having a look around. I want to make sure there aren't any traps."

Jane grimaced.

"Only joking!" I said. I felt my phone vibrate and saw that Wick had sent me a text. "Oh."

"What's wrong?"

My heart sank. "Oh, nothing. Nothing at all."

Wick wasn't coming. He said that he really wanted to, but

thought it would be best to avoid a certain gentleman. I glared over at Darcy, who was in a corner with Charles and Caroline.

Any hope I had for a wonderful evening quickly dissolved. Now I was stuck in a room full of people who despised my very existence. Instead of hanging out with Wick, I would have to brace myself for whatever was going to come my way.

"Are you sure you're okay?" Jane looked concerned.

"Yes, fine," I lied. I didn't want to ruin her evening.

A waiter came over with a silver tray filled with wontons and egg rolls.

"Yum." Lydia grabbed a handful of food. "So much better than the crap they serve in the dining hall." She made a disgusted face as she shoved an entire egg roll in her mouth.

Jane sighed.

"Hey!" Charles approached us with a huge smile on his face. "Thanks for coming." He kissed Jane lightly on the cheek before hugging both me and Lydia.

While Jane chose to never see the bad side of people, I sincerely believed that Charles didn't have a bad side. He even put up with Lydia's incessant questions about the party, the food, the private room — I was surprised she didn't ask him to open up his wallet so she could see how much cash he was carrying.

While Lydia played twenty inappropriate questions, I started looking around to see who was there. The standard cash cliques were in their respective groups, but I did catch a few of the Longbourn girls whispering and looking at us. I looked down at my outfit, but realized that I could be dressed head to toe in designer clothing and they'd still look at me with disdain. I was a reminder that there was life outside the precious little bubble they lived in. And I knew that they despised me for many things, but most of all for thriving despite their best efforts to bring me down.

I brought my attention back to my group and could see Jane's eyes getting wider every time Lydia opened her mouth.

"Charlotte's here," I said, nodding toward the door. "And Lydia, they just brought out something that looks like quesadillas."

As I thought she would, Lydia homed in on the server and mercifully left us.

I leaned in closer to Jane and whispered, "Have fun with Charles. I'll keep an eye on Lydia."

Jane smiled gratefully and went over to a group of couches with Charles. I waved Charlotte over, but Colin, mistaking that my enthusiasm was for him, approached as well.

"Hello, Elizabeth," he said. "It is a pleasure to see you here, and dressed in such a pleasing manner. What blend is that fabric?"

"Yeah, uh, nice seeing you as well."

He leaned in and put his hand on the small of my back. "Elizabeth, do you think I could persuade you to join me on the dance floor?"

"Oh, um. Have you met Charlotte Lucas?"

Charlotte and Colin exchanged pleasantries. I was hoping this distraction would keep me from dancing with Colin.

"So, shall we?" Colin motioned toward the platform where a few couples were moving to a slightly slow song.

I couldn't think of a good excuse, so I decided that I may as well get it over with. I walked with Colin to the dance floor and, once there, he awkwardly grabbed my waist and I cautiously lowered my arms around his shoulders. I didn't realize until we were standing there that he was a couple inches shorter than me.

He started to move and stepped on my foot. "Oh, I'm so sorry," he said, staring at our steps as if they were a math problem he could solve.

"That's okay." I started to move back and forth, trying to not make my movements too sudden.

"Well, you certainly are a good dancer."

"Thanks."

"You know, Elizabeth, you can play the piano, dance, are smart enough to get a scholarship and, might I add, make a mean latte. Is there anything you can't do?"

I forced out a laugh. "Oh, you know . . ."

"Know what?"

"Sorry?"

"You were saying, *you know*. What am I supposed to know?" Colin looked at me expectantly. I didn't have anything to say. And I wasn't one hundred percent sure, but I think Colin was under the horrible impression that I was flirting with him.

My back stiffened. "No, nothing. Sorry."

He nodded. "No, no, it should be me who apologizes. I simply misunderstood. It is something that can happen easily, especially when the music is playing at such high decibels."

"That's okay."

"Once again, Elizabeth, you are too gracious."

"Uh, thanks."

"You are more than welcome."

I tried to avoid any more awkward exchanges by pretending I was enthralled by a painting that hung on the wall behind Colin until the song thankfully ended, allowing me an escape from my misery.

"Having fun?" Charlotte laughed as I approached.

"Tons. You?"

She shrugged. "These things have gotten easier for me —" Charlotte bit her lip. She had always felt guilty that the torture she endured became less severe when I'd arrived on campus. I was fresh meat.

She tried to smile. "Plus, the food's good." She held up a mini-burger.

"That does look good. I —"

Darcy was suddenly in front of us. "Hello."

"Uh, hi."

"I was hoping that you could join me for a dance."

I was completely shocked by his invitation. When I didn't respond, he said, "I'll see you in a moment." And with that, he walked away.

"Wait a second." I looked at Charlotte. "Did Will Darcy just ask me to dance?"

Charlotte's mouth dropped open. "*That's* Will Darcy? Lizzie, he's hot."

"What?"

"That guy" — she motioned her head in his direction — "is hot."

"Are you crazy?"

"He really must have made a bad impression on you if you can't see that not only is he gorgeous, but that he obviously has a thing for you."

"Oh, please . . ."

Charlotte paused. "And I think you have a thing for him."

"What?"

She laughed. "If you don't have any feelings for Will Darcy, why are you blushing and fixing your hair?"

I pulled my hands away from my hair. "Okay, you've clearly lost your mind. There is nothing going on between me and Darcy. Obviously, he's setting me up for something."

"Lizzie!"

"I'm serious. Plus, he asked and then just disappeared. He's planning something."

"Yeah, well, he's heading over here again."

Darcy stared intently at me and nodded toward the dance floor before walking over there.

I looked at Charlotte. "Am I supposed to follow him?"

Charlotte pushed me. "Will you just go already?!"

I was in a daze as I got on the dance floor. It was like having an out-of-body experience. I found myself going through the motions, but also looking around trying to figure out where the ambush was coming from. Darcy slipped his arms around me, with much more ease than Colin had, and before I knew it, we were in something approximating an embrace. Darcy was several inches taller than me, and he leaned his head down so our eyes locked.

I was face-to-face with the enemy.

"I see you made it home safe the other night," he said.

"Yes. I'm touched by your concern for my safety."

I broke away from his stare, but ended up being greeted by dozens of eyeballs transfixed on us. At first I thought they were waiting for something to happen. But then I noticed the jealousy on the girls' faces. And outrage. It seemed that not a single girl in the room could believe that Pemberley's most eligible student would be slumming with me.

"You know" — I turned back to him — "working has many benefits. It's a really great way to make new friends."

Darcy clenched his jaw. "Ah yes, George Wickham. He's really good at making new friends. *Retaining* them, however, has always been a challenge for him."

"I'm sure he cries himself to sleep every night, thinking about losing such a wonderful friend as you. How will he ever recover?"

Darcy greeted my response with silence. We swayed to the music for the remainder of the song. When I thought I was going to be free, he tightened his grip around my waist. A new song began.

"So, what kind of music do you like to listen to for fun?" Darcy asked out of nowhere.

"Excuse me?"

"I thought I'd change the subject."

"Oh. Were we discussing something you weren't comfortable with?"

"No, I was just trying to see if there was something we could talk about that wouldn't end up in an argument."

"Ah. Good luck with that."

"Yes, apparently I'm going to need it."

His attempt at being friendly unnerved me.

"You know," I said, "I can't figure you out at all."

"Really? Are you finding yourself thinking a lot about me, then?"

The conceit, again! "Hardly. But you don't seem to make any sense."

"And you do?" He smirked.

"At least I'm consistent."

"And I'm not consistent?"

I thought for a moment. "No, I guess you are." I stepped back from him and pulled my arms away. "You said that you think I have a problem with people with money. But I think you have a problem with people *without* money."

He looked down at the floor. "You're right. You don't understand me at all."

"Well, I guess we're a lost cause." I turned my back on him

and walked off the dance floor. I tried to not seem desperate as I looked for Charlotte in the cluster of people around the room.

I felt a tug on my arm. It was Caroline, who was with Cat. "What do you think you're doing?" she asked accusingly.

"I don't know what you mean," I said.

She looked disgusted. "I heard from Jane that you've been hanging around with George Wickham."

"So?"

Her lip curled up. "So? He's not to be trusted."

"I'm sorry, Caroline, but I really doubt you have any concern about who I hang out with or my well-being."

"I couldn't care less about your well-being," she admitted. "But I do care about Darcy. The mere mention of Wick upsets him. After everything Wick has done to him."

"What *Wick* has done?"

Caroline grabbed my arm tightly. "We don't want him around, okay? We heard that his little group was thinking of coming by tonight. Believe me, we put a stop to that. And to think that my brother and I have been nothing but kind to you. You only think about yourself, don't you?"

"Caroline." I spoke slowly so that, hopefully, one of us could start understanding the other. "I don't know what you are talking about. Yes, *Charles* has been very kind to me. I know there are issues between Darcy and Wick, but why should that matter to me? It's not like I'm friends with Darcy . . . or you. Who I hang out with isn't really any of your business."

"Suit yourself." Caroline walked away.

I went to find Jane, but Cat blocked my path.

"You know, scum, for someone who claims to have no interest in Darcy, you seem to spend enough time with him."

I turned and walked away. Jane was waving me down from the other side of the room.

"Lizzie!" She approached me with a worried look. "What was *that* all about?"

Even Jane knew something had to be off if Caroline and Cat were speaking to me. Especially Caroline — her influence over her brother and his unexplained respect for her were the only things about him that I didn't like.

After I relayed the exchange, Jane sighed. "Lizzie, I haven't been hearing good things about George Wickham. You should be careful."

"Not you too." I didn't like that Jane would take Caroline and Darcy's side.

"It's not that. I asked Charles, and he said that the story Wick told you was an absolute lie."

"Yeah, but whatever information he got was from Darcy. So, in my book, it shouldn't be trusted."

Jane looked over at Charles. "I don't know, Lizzie. Charles couldn't tell me exactly what happened because he made a promise to Darcy, but he really doesn't have a reason to lie to me."

"I know, I know. . . ."

"JANE!" Lydia barreled over to us. "I'm having so much fun. Can you believe I'm the only freshman here? Like, this totally has to be a huge mark for my social standing. And, can you just imagine, I mean, what if *I* get asked to prom, too?" Lydia screeched so loudly that half of the room turned around to glare.

"Lydia," Jane whispered. "Please."

Lydia didn't hear her. Or, more likely, chose to ignore her.

"Caroline!" Lydia shouted to a stunned Caroline. "So, like, during spring break, we're going to Vera's for our prom dresses. I mean, for Jane's dress. Do you know if a freshman has ever gone to prom? Like, ever?"

Caroline looked at Lydia with even more disgust than she usually reserved for me.

"No," she said dismissively. "Prom is for *junior* women at Longbourn. While it is tradition for most of the women to be taken by men from Pemberley, some exceptions are made." She shot a look at me. "But any straying from custom is frowned upon."

"Do you want to come with us to Vera's?"

"I will be spending my vacation in Greece."

Lydia squealed again. "That's so awesome."

Caroline nodded coldly.

"I mean, I wish we were going somewhere, but no . . ." Lydia started sulking. "Like, Daddy got millions in his buyout, so the fact that we can't go somewhere *fabulous* like Greece is so unfair."

"Lydia!" Jane stood up and pulled her sister away from Caroline. "Enough!"

The majority of the students on our side of the room had heard everything Lydia had said.

"I'm just having fun," Lydia protested. "You're so uptight." Her eyes grew wide and she started jumping up and down. "No. *Way.* This song was, like, THE song from camp last summer. I totally remember the routine we came up with." An up-tempo pop song started playing on the sound system, and before any of us could stop her, Lydia was on the dance floor, spinning around with her arms stretched out. In less than ten seconds, she cleared a space of about ten feet around her. She was relishing the attention.

Jane was horrified. "Please make her stop." Her voice was nearly inaudible.

I headed over to the platform. Lydia was doing something that looked like the Charleston, but with her usual manic energy. She started spinning her fists in the air and shouting "WOO!" every few seconds. I could hear the snickering as I passed through the crowd.

"Um, Lydia." I got as close to the platform as I could safely get without bringing too much attention to myself or getting kicked in the face by Lydia's current attempt to channel a Rockette.

The performance was pure agony to watch. How Lydia could've thought she was impressing people was beyond me. I wanted to look away, but it was one of those horrifying scenes that you just can't take your eyes off of. Just when I thought it couldn't get worse, she did jazz hands. Full-on, Broadway-style jazz hands.

When the song was over, Lydia took a deep bow. A few of the guys started whistling while the majority of the Longbourn girls were laughing. A few had even recorded the dance on their phones.

Poor, poor Jane.

"Oh!" Lydia exclaimed when the next song came on. I quickly grabbed her arm. "Lizzie, let me go!" she protested.

I ignored her and dragged her along until Colin stepped in my path.

"Why, Lydia, that was delightful," he said.

"Thanks!" she replied.

"You really have such a great enthusiasm. I haven't seen leaps like that since an evening I spent at the Joffrey Ballet during fall break last year. I remember that time of year so well because it was unseasonably warm. The program was a delightful one — you may have enjoyed it yourself. . . ."

Colin was making things worse. What we needed was to get Lydia out of there, but Colin was prolonging the embarrassment by giving a detailed review of her performance.

Finally, Jane couldn't take it anymore. She rushed over, grabbed Lydia, and walked her outside.

"Oh, well . . ." Colin was taken aback by Lydia's abrupt departure. "So, Elizabeth, dare we take the dance floor again in hopes of repeating that splendid performance given by Lydia?" There wasn't an ounce of sarcasm in his voice. He was being completely sincere.

"I . . ." I glanced at the door. I really needed to go help Jane. Or possibly prevent a murder.

Fortunately, Charlotte came to the rescue. "Colin, I was hoping you could tell me more about your family's sailboat." While Charlotte was getting an earful, I dashed outside. Jane was sitting on the curb, shivering.

"Jane," I said, "it's freezing out here. Come inside."

"I can't. I'm so humiliated."

"Where's Lydia?"

"I don't know — and, honestly, I don't care. She ran off when I was trying to reason with her. She has zero respect for me, our family, our school, Charles. . . ."

I didn't know what to say. I would do anything for Jane, but I couldn't turn back time.

"I want to go home," she said.

I headed back inside to get our things at the coat check.

Charles approached me. "Lizzie, is Jane okay?"

I handed our tickets over to the coat check person. "Yes, she's fine. She . . . uh, she has a bit of a headache, so we're going to head home. It was really a great party, Charles. Thanks so much for inviting us."

Before Charles had a chance to respond, the girl at the coat check handed me Jane's coat. She bit her lip. "Um, the other coat isn't back here."

"I gave you the ticket."

Her cheeks became flushed. "I know, but that hanger's empty."

"What?"

Charles grabbed both tickets from her hand and went behind the counter to look for my coat. But I had a sinking feeling that he wasn't going to find it.

"What's going on?" Colin came over, with Darcy behind him.

"Nothing," I said.

"This is ridiculous!" Charles exclaimed. "How could someone just walk off with somebody else's coat? I want to see the manager."

The girl looked nervous. "That's not necessary. What did it look like?"

"It was a gray peacoat, it came above my knees. . . ."

The girl's eyes grew wide. "What brand?"

I looked back toward Colin and Darcy. "It was Old Navy."

"Oh . . ." The color drained from the girl's face.

"What do you mean, 'oh'?" Charles was furious. This was the first time I'd ever seen him angry. And I also realized that he was standing up for me. My bottom lip started to quiver. I was used to being attacked, not defended.

"Some girls came over a few minutes ago to get their coats and one of them said she'd lost her claim and identified the coat. And, well, I didn't think . . ." The girl was embarrassed. I knew what she was going to say: When there were all these expensive designer coats in the room, who would lie about having such a nonglamorous item of clothing?

"Just forget about it." I tried to keep my voice even.

"Lizzie, I'm so sorry." Charles was aghast.

"I'm going to go. . . ."

Colin started to take off his blazer. "Here, at least take my jacket."

Charles took out his wallet. "You have to let me pay you for it. I'm horrified that something like this happened at my party. I can't believe it."

The thing was, I could believe it. Something had to happen this evening. I couldn't attend a party without some sort of humiliation. All along, I'd assumed somebody was going to throw something at me, or trip me, or set my hair on fire. But instead, they'd stolen from me. And not because they wanted what I had. Simply because they could.

I quickly waved away Colin's and Charles's generous offers and went into the winter night unprotected. The freezing cold was a reminder that things were never going to get easier.

13.

I SPENT THE NEXT DAY AT WORK REPLAYING THE EVENING IN my head. All I had left were questions. What had Wick done last night instead of being with me? Would the pranks against me ever end? Would Lydia's behavior — or her disclosure about their father — affect Jane and her prospects? Were people really going to be so shallow and judgmental?

Unfortunately, I already knew *that* answer.

I raced out of the café the second my shift was over . . . and found an unexpected visitor waiting for me outside.

Colin.

"Elizabeth, did you find your jacket?" He motioned toward Jane's red wool coat, which I was now going to be wearing until the end of winter.

"Unfortunately, no."

"Oh, I am sorry to hear that. I once lost a jacket that I loved very much. It was corduroy. No, tweed. Brownish gray. Really, it was a fine coat. My teddy bear had a matching one. We often wore them together. But then, one day, I left it in a park. When my mother and I went back for it, it was . . . gone."

"I can see you miss it," I said, looking for an escape route.

"Anyway," Colin continued, "I was wondering if I might speak with you for a moment."

"Sure." I sat down next to him on the bench.

"There are certain rites of passage that I think are a very important part of becoming an adult."

He looked at me expectedly. I was so tired, all I could do was nod.

"Prom is one of those rites." My stomach dropped. "It is a momentous occasion, especially for a Longbourn girl like yourself, and I believe that we'd make a great match to attend. Obviously, we have the dancing part down." He let out a small laugh. "And I know with your circumstances you may have some difficulty with the dress, but I would be more than willing to pay for your accoutrements if that would make you more comfortable. I . . ." Colin's prim stature faltered for a moment and he seemed to be at a loss for words. No doubt this was the first time such a thing had ever happened to him. "I . . . I do find you most appealing. I've never met anybody like you before. You certainly are someone that I've always found very curious." I knew that I should've probably taken this as a compliment, but the way he said it, I couldn't help but think he found me more interesting as an oddity in his rich world than someone he found attractive. "We can obviously work out all the details at a later date, but I thought it would be best to move forward with our plans."

"Oh." I looked down at my gloves. "Thank you for thinking of me."

"No problem. We'll be in touch." Colin started walking away.

"Wait!" I called out after him. "I didn't give you an answer!"

His face fell. "Well, I just assumed . . ."

"Well, you shouldn't. While I'm very honored that you'd want to take me to prom, I'm going to have to decline."

Colin laughed. "Oh, I know this game. Playing hard to get, are we?"

"No, we're not."

"Oh, Elizabeth, I know how girls like you are. You want to be pursued first. Very well, I'm game. You set out your rabbit, and I'll get my hounds. It could be fun."

"No, Colin." I stood up and bent down slightly so I could look him in the eye. "Again, I'm very flattered, but I'm not playing hard to get. My response won't change. I'm sorry, but the answer is, and will always be, no."

I hated being so direct with him, but he'd left me no choice.

Colin looked thoughtful for a minute. "This is why I like you so much, Elizabeth. You're unpredictable. I know we'll have a great time."

"Apparently, you aren't hearing me."

Colin sighed. "I do hear you, but — and please know that I do not mean any disrespect — do you really think with your circumstances that you'll be getting other offers?"

His bluntness shocked me.

"No," I said, "I'm sure I won't. But I know that prom here is probably something that I wouldn't enjoy, and you should really go with someone who you'd have fun with."

"I have every confidence that next time I discuss this with you, your answer will be different."

"No, Colin. Please tell me if there's anything I'm doing right now to make you think that there will be another answer.

Because if you let me know, I will correct it so you can ask somebody else."

"Oh, Elizabeth, you really *are* something else."

I stood there with my mouth wide open. Colin was one of the smartest students in his class, but apparently he was lacking in common sense. He squeezed my shoulder and walked away.

How much clearer could I have been?

14.

I FOUND CHARLOTTE IN MY ROOM WHEN I GOT BACK.

"Oh, good — you're finally here!" she exclaimed before I even had the door halfway open.

"Well, I had a visitor. What's that?"

On my bed was a giant silver box with a red ribbon around it.

"We don't know." Jane jumped up from her seat. "That's why we've been dying for you to come home. It was delivered an hour ago."

"But I didn't order . . . What on earth?"

"Open it!" Charlotte grabbed the box and put it in my arms. "I want to see who it's from!"

Jane laughed. "And I want to know what it *is*."

I sat down on my bed and untied the red ribbon. Inside the silver box was white tissue. I lifted up the paper to find a beautiful gray winter coat. I looked at the tag and was shocked by the designer's name.

"Who sent this?" I asked. I took the coat out of the box and started looking for a card. Or receipt. Or even a tag that would have given me a hint where the jacket came from.

Jane was sifting through the tissue on the floor to see if she could find anything.

"Jane?"

She looked up. "It wasn't from me. Maybe Charles . . . but why wouldn't he have sent a card? Or said something to me about it?"

Then my stomach turned. I knew whom it was from and it made me feel so awful.

"It's from Colin."

"How do you know?" Charlotte asked.

"Because he just asked me to prom."

"What?" they said in unison.

"And I said no." I filled them in on the details of Colin's proposal. Even how honest and somewhat rude I was to him.

"I can't believe you aren't going to go," Charlotte said. "Besides, it was thoughtful of him to offer to buy your dress . . . and now the coat."

"I know. I can't keep this. It's too much. And it isn't like I have anything against Colin. He's so nice." I looked down at the coat. "*And* generous. It's about prom at Longbourn. I'm not going to sit here and fool myself that I'd be welcome at prom. Look at what happens when I go to a regular party. Plus, I want to go to something like that with somebody special."

Charlotte shrugged. "I would be disappointed if I didn't go. But Colin's right, you and I are tainted goods."

"Charlotte!" Jane was horrified. "I can't believe you would say such a thing. At least you two don't have a sister who humiliated you in front of the entire world!"

"Oh, I didn't realize the entire world fit into the restaurant last night," I teased. "And to think, I missed an opportunity to meet the president of the United States."

"I'm just glad I didn't run into my ex-boyfriend," Charlotte continued.

"Apparently, you guys haven't seen the latest Internet sensation?"

Jane pulled up a video of Lydia's dance that someone had uploaded. "The family is so proud."

"Oh, Jane . . ." I started scrolling through the hate-filled comments. "I'm so sorry."

She shook her head. "I'm going to try to get over it. Someday."

"It's nice to have goals."

My cell phone went off. My heart jumped when I saw it was Wick. "Hey," I said, moving into the hallway for some privacy.

"So, you're talking to me even after I left you alone with the trust-fund babies last night?" His voice was warm and friendly.

"I guess I could see my way to forgive you."

"You're so generous. That's very un-Longbourn of you. Be careful, you might get kicked out next."

"At least then I'd be in better company."

A tingle went up my spine as he laughed. "Listen, I'm sorry for bailing, especially at the last minute. I really wanted to go and had every intention of being there. But last night as I got ready, I knew that if I showed up it wouldn't be good for you. There's no way that I could be in the same room as you-know-who, and I didn't want to bring any negative attention to you."

"I understand. I don't like being in the same room with him, either."

Charlotte suddenly exited our room. "Lizzie . . . Jane needs you."

"Listen, can I call you back?"

"You better."

I ran back into our room and found Jane curled up on her bed.

"Jane, what's wrong? You know nobody will be talking about that stupid video in a week."

"No, it's not that." She handed me her phone. There was a text from Charles.

Can't make it tonight. Things are hectic. I'll be in touch.

"Oh." I didn't know what to say. It seemed very unlike Charles to break off a date, and to be so terse in doing it. He was completely smitten with Jane. He'd spent most of his party at her side and doted on her. "I'm sure it's nothing. Let's go grab dinner."

As Jane and Charlotte got ready, I quickly called Wick back and explained the situation. I was not at all surprised when he said he completely understood. When they were set, I hung up and together we headed down the long staircase toward the dining hall.

Caroline was heading out the main entrance door with Cat. When Caroline saw us, she turned to Cat and said loudly, "I'm *so* glad you're coming out tonight with us. I really think you and Charles will hit it off." Jane stopped dead in her tracks. Caroline continued, "You know how important it is to protect your family name. When you're a Bingley, like a de Bourgh, you have to be careful about the people you associate with. I would think that most Longbourn girls would know that well." She glanced toward us. "Or at least the ones who have a reputation worth preserving."

Cat nodded absently as Caroline walked out. Cat followed obediently behind her.

"Jane . . ."

The color rushed out of Jane's face. "So that's it. I've been replaced."

"That's ridiculous. I'm sure there's an explanation for —"

Jane turned around and headed back upstairs. "I'm not hungry."

"Jane!" I rushed after her. "Anybody who has ever seen you two together knows that Charles is crazy about you. Please, if Darcy looked at Caroline with even *half* the affection that Charles looks at you, she'd be walking around campus with her prom dress on."

Jane smiled. "Really?"

"Are you kidding me? There's no way that he's going to be able to stay away from you."

15.

I'D BEEN WRONG ABOUT A LOT OF THINGS IN MY LIFE. BUT one thing that I would have bet my life savings on (as paltry as the sum may have been) was that Charles would be back to pursuing Jane in a matter of days.

But I was wrong. Dead wrong.

Two weeks passed, and nothing. It was heartbreaking to watch Jane stare at her cell phone, wishing it to ring. She wasn't the only one confused by Charles dropping off the face of the earth. It didn't make sense.

And to add to the list of boys with confusing behaviors, Colin refused to admit that he'd bought me the coat, and had dropped off the face of the earth as well. Or at least he'd stopped visiting me at the Junction.

And then there was Wick. Wick would visit me occasionally at work and flirt (at least I thought he was flirting), but he hadn't asked me out on another date.

What made it even worse was that Valentine's Day was approaching. And if there was anything more annoying than a Longbourn girl obsessing over prom, it was a Longbourn girl freaking out over Valentine's Day. Especially since I'd found out that Valentine's Day was the most popular day for Pemberley boys to ask Longbourn girls to prom.

It was bad enough to see the red balloons and heart signs sprouting up in town and infiltrating campus. I was trying to shield Jane from all the puppy love as much as possible. That night, I even volunteered to run to the dining hall to grab us dinner, for fear they'd be serving a red meal on heart-shaped plates. I ran into Charlotte on the way there.

"Oh, hi." She seemed unnerved to see me. "Heading to dinner?"

As we walked down the staircase, I saw Colin waiting in the entrance hall. "Oh, no. What does he want? Can he not take a hint?"

"Lizzie." Charlotte slowed down. "He's here for me."

"Oh." I tried to not sound so shocked.

"I didn't know when to tell you, but I'm going to prom with Colin."

I laughed. "Are you joking?"

Charlotte's face fell. "No, I'm not. Are you shocked that he could recover from your rejection?"

"No, not at all." I didn't know which one of us should have been more offended — her for my thinking she was second to me, or me for Charlotte's thinking I'd be so egotistical. "I know you really want to go to prom, and I couldn't be happier for you. Really."

Charlotte smiled weakly. "I don't blame you for being surprised, but I'm not a romantic, Lizzie. I'm practical. I want to go to prom, and he asked."

"I'm sure you are going to have a great time. I can't wait to see your dress."

"Thanks. Well, I better . . ."

"Of course, have a great night."

I watched Charlotte as she ran down to greet Colin, who had a heart-shaped box of chocolates hidden behind his back. They both seemed happy, albeit a little awkward with each other. Colin tried to go in for a double kiss on the cheek, but ended up kissing Charlotte's ear.

I went to the dining hall, collecting food to take back to the room. Since the "Lydia Incident" (Lydia, of course, wasn't embarrassed about the video; she was happy that people knew who she was), both Jane and I had been going through the motions.

The upcoming long weekend for Presidents' Day was a welcome respite. Most of the campus would be empty. While my parents were hoping I would come visit, I wanted to get my work done and knew the Java Junction would be slow, so it would be a great way for me to earn money *and* get some reading done.

Plus, Mrs. Gardiner had a surprise for me that Friday during my piano lesson.

"I think it is time we had a little chat about the spring recital," she said. She had a mischievous grin on her face, which I knew meant trouble.

I nodded. "I assumed I'd be playing the Rachmaninoff." We'd been working on the eighteenth variation of Rhapsody on a Theme of Paganini.

"Yes, I think you should play it — but the whole thing, with the orchestra. You'd be the featured performer."

I was stunned into silence. The entire Rhapsody was nearly twenty-five minutes long. "I don't think . . ."

Mrs. Gardiner got up from her chair beside the piano in the music suite. "You aren't going to be able to do it if you *don't think* you can do it. You can! And you will!"

This was why I was at Longbourn, to challenge myself. She was right. I needed to believe in myself.

"Elizabeth, I've never had a student as gifted as you. I want your performance to be the wonderful coda of the year."

"Okay." I flipped through the entire piece, studying the runs. "I can do this."

She clapped her hands together. "Excellent! That's the spirit I was looking for. I was getting worried about you."

"Why were you worried about me?"

Mrs. Gardiner gave me a weak smile. "You just haven't seemed like yourself the last couple of days. I know you have had some difficulty adjusting, but you seemed to finally get your stride."

"Oh," I replied. I couldn't think of anything else to say. I'd always tried to leave whatever was going on in my personal life behind during my lessons — but clearly I hadn't done the best job of it.

"I don't mean to pry," she said apologetically.

Most teachers at Longbourn enjoyed the student gossip as much as the girls. But Mrs. Gardiner was the only teacher who seemed to be looking out for me.

"It's fine," I told her. "It's just that my friend is going through a hard time right now."

"Okay, dear." She patted me on the back. "Have a good long weekend. And by a good long weekend, I mean you should practice as much as you can. This piece is going to be a killer."

I was happy for the distraction. Diving into a challenging arrangement would give me something to do besides sit in silence with Jane each night. I would be studying and she would have a book in front of her, but I was pretty sure she wasn't studying. To make matters worse, her mother still insisted they go in for a consultation on her prom dress over the break. The last thing Jane needed was a reminder of what had happened — or, in her case, what *hadn't* happened — with Charles.

16.

THE CAMPUS WAS QUIET ALL WEEKEND. I WAS ONE OF THE few people who remained in the dorm. Even Charlotte went home to Maine. I should've been used to an isolated existence at this point, but I really missed Jane. And Charlotte, even though things had been a little uncomfortable between us since she agreed to go to prom with Colin.

I worked Monday afternoon, since we didn't have class. It began picking up in the late afternoon as students started returning to campus.

"Miss me?" a familiar voice called out as my back was to the counter.

"Where were you this weekend?" I asked Wick. I was disappointed that I hadn't seen or heard from him.

"In Manhattan." He playfully pulled on my visor.

"Oh, big-city boy, are we?" I started making his regular drink. "And what were you doing there?"

"You know, the usual."

"Causing trouble?"

"Only for the people who deserve it."

Even though I was annoyed that he hadn't told me he'd be away, I couldn't hold a grudge against him. We were too much alike.

"Lizzie!" Lydia ran up to the counter. "I'm so happy to see you. This weekend was awful — Jane still hasn't forgiven me. She's being so unreasonable." She paused for a brief second. "I want a tall, frozen mocha latte with extra whipped cream and chocolate."

I grimaced. Lydia knew what a pain those frozen drinks were. But she didn't care. And why should she? This was my job, after all.

As I scooped out the ice, Lydia turned her attention toward Wick. "Hey," she said as she eyed him up and down. "You go to Pemberley?"

"Lydia," I interrupted. "This is Wick."

A smile slowly spread on her face. "Oh, you're the one who got kicked out of Pemberley and are mortal enemies with Darcy."

"Lydia!" I was surprised by how much I sounded like Jane when I scolded her.

Wick just laughed. "My, aren't we forward? That's okay, I like forward."

I turned on the blender so I could drown out Lydia's excessive gabbing. I selfishly wanted to have Wick all to myself and take a break so we could catch up, but there was no way Lydia would be leaving us alone.

Lydia grabbed her drink out of my hand before I even had a chance to put the lid on. She started playing with the straw in what I could have only assumed was supposed to be a seductive manner.

"When's your break?" Wick asked me.

I glanced at the clock. "I suppose I could take a few minutes now." We headed toward a table. Lydia followed.

"You know," Lydia cooed to Wick, "I think Darcy probably hates Lizzie more than he hates you."

"Thanks for that." I shot her a look.

"What? Isn't that what you guys talk about? Darcy?"

Wick shrugged his shoulders. "You might not believe this, but there are things in this world worth talking about other than Will Darcy."

"Exactly." In fact, Wick and I hardly ever talked about Darcy. There was no need to bring up such an unpleasant subject.

"So, do you have a girlfriend?" Lydia asked bluntly.

"Why, are you auditioning?" Wick teased.

"You shouldn't encourage her," I whispered in his ear.

He raised his eyebrows. "Lydia, you can do much better than a guy like me."

"Oh, I don't know." Lydia bit her straw. "I like bad boys."

I resisted every urge to vomit. I was questioning humanity enough because of how Charles had treated Jane, and the last thing I needed to witness was flirting between Lydia and Wick.

"Well, I'm sorry, but this bad boy is somewhat taken at the moment." Wick winked at me.

I felt my face grow hot by his attention, and what he was implying.

"With whom?" Lydia asked.

"Oh." Wick wiggled in his seat. "She goes to Longbourn, so you might know her."

I looked down at the floor, embarrassed.

"Who?" Lydia prodded, not getting it.

"Sylvia Kent. She's a senior."

Sylvia Kent.

Sylvia Kent?

Sylvia Kent!

I tried to process what he was saying. I knew who Sylvia Kent was, but it didn't make sense. I thought he despised the girls at Longbourn just as much as I did. I was trying to understand, but there was a part of my brain that just wasn't letting me. *Sylvia Kent?*

Wick could tell with one look at me that there was something wrong. I'm sure I wasn't being very subtle with my confusion, but Wick knew me. We had an understanding between us — or at least I thought we had, until the words "Sylvia Kent" left his lips.

He turned to Lydia. "It's Lydia, right?" he asked. She became overly pleased that he knew her name. "Could you give me a few minutes alone with Lizzie?"

Lydia got up, went to an empty table, and started texting.

I couldn't look at Wick. I was so horrified that I'd assumed he had any feeling for me at all.

"I'm sorry I didn't say anything to you sooner," he began.

I cut him off. "Oh, it's fine. You didn't need to say anything to me. It's not like we were, um, dating or anything."

He leaned back in his chair. "I don't want you to be mad at me — I *do* have an ulterior motive with Sylvia. Her dad runs a pretty big law firm in New York. Entertainment law, not nearly as prestigious as Mr. Darcy's corporate law office. But since that didn't work out, I thought I'd try to make a connection a different way. An internship at his law firm practically guarantees acceptance at an Ivy League school."

I was trying to reconcile everything Wick had said to me in the past about the spoiled brats at Pemberley and Longbourn with what he was saying now.

He continued, "I know that I must seem like a hypocrite to you. That's why I didn't want to tell you. But you're still fairly new to the whole rich crowd. Lizzie, you've got to understand that we need to take advantage of our situations when we can. Hang around with them long enough, you start to appreciate it, even as you work to undermine it. There's a big difference between *connections* and *connection*. What I have with Sylvia is a matter of *connections*. What I have with you is a matter of *connection*. One is vastly more important than the other, and I'm sure you can imagine which it is."

All I could do was nod. I excused myself and went to the back room. I was equal parts hurt, angry, and embarrassed by his revelation. I really liked Wick, and I'd foolishly thought he liked me.

Maybe, in a twisted way, he still did. But what really did matter most — connections or connection? He was the first guy I met here who'd understood me. He liked me for who I was. But was that enough? After all, I didn't have a rich family or fancy job prospects.

He hadn't once mentioned that he *liked* Sylvia. Did that mean he could still like me? Or that liking had nothing to do with it? Could I truly fault him for taking advantage, when I knew that neither of us would ever be *given* an advantage?

I looked at my gray coat hanging on the employee coatrack. Colin still refused to admit he bought it for me, so I couldn't have returned it even if I wanted to. But even though I knew that, I wondered: Did keeping the coat mean that I was taking advantage of my situation? Did I feel the same way about Charlotte going to the prom with Colin that I did about Wick and Sylvia?

It was bad enough to see friendship and love in terms of politics. But seeing it in terms of business was even worse. I looked out from the back room and saw Wick patiently waiting for me. Then he looked up. Saw me. And we hung there for a moment.

I knew I was overreacting to what he'd said because I wanted him to like me. I was taking it personally.

The question was: How personal did it really get? Was I frightened by his desire for connections, or by my own lack of them?

I stayed there in the doorway until he got the hint and left.

It's very easy to get a boy to leave a room.

It's much harder to get him to leave your thoughts.

17.

HE FOLLOWING WEEKS BECAME A CYCLE OF SCHOOL, homework, practice, and work. The pranks and vitriol lessened as students started studying for midterms and the prom committee called meetings practically every evening. The piano had become the only bright spot in my day. I felt like I was accomplishing something, *anything* by making my way, slowly yet surely, through Rachmaninoff.

Jane and I stayed in most nights. She became more and more depressed as the list of girls with prom dates grew and grew.

Adding insult to injury, she was having a very expensive dress made for her. Her mother seemed to think that everything would eventually work out, and didn't want her to be unprepared.

Neither one of us even bothered to attend the "mandatory" prom orientation meeting where the rundown of activities was discussed, media release forms were handed out, and preinterviews were scheduled. (Charlotte decided to brave the meeting, only to be told the wrong room. Then, when she finally arrived, they claimed they didn't have any more forms for her.)

I had even begun looking forward to work more, as it was my only real social interaction during the week. Wick didn't come in nearly as much anymore. Being around each other was suddenly awkward. For the first time since I'd met him, I felt censored. I couldn't be open around him and tell him what I wanted to say: *Why her? Why not me?* But we both already knew the answer to those questions.

While Wick stayed away, another presence emerged. Much to my dismay, Darcy began making regular appearances during my shift. I tried to avoid any conversation with him besides inquiries into his beverage selection.

"I think that guy has a thing for you," Tara said one day, motioning to Darcy.

"Hardly," I replied. "He despises me. Although probably not as much as I detest him."

Tara smirked. "My, we certainly have strong feelings for someone, don't we? Are you sure you detest him, or is it something else?"

"Please."

"Well, he only sits down with his coffee when you're here. When you aren't, he leaves."

"Believe me, he's only doing it to punish me."

The punishment continued for another couple weeks. Finally, nearly a month after Charles's party, he caught up with me on my way home. He was with a guy in his late twenties.

Darcy and his friend joined me on the sidewalk. "Hi, Lizzie," Darcy said, as if we'd just happened to encounter each other. "We're heading over in your direction — do you mind if we walk with you?"

"I'm Will Fitzpatrick," the guy said to me. "It's my ten-year reunion at Pemberley. I'm just visiting my little cousin before heading to our party."

"Hi," I replied. He had a friendly disposition, very opposite to Darcy.

"Fitz, this is Elizabeth Bennet," Darcy said, making the proper introduction.

"Please call me Fitz — all my friends do. With two Wills in the family, it just made it easier for everybody to refer to us by our last names."

I smiled politely, although I wasn't really interested in why everybody called Darcy by that name, and not Will.

"I've heard a lot about you," Fitz said warmly.

"That's unfortunate," I replied. "I can assure you that I'm not nearly as awful as your cousin has made me out to be."

Fitz laughed. "Awful? Quite the opposite. He only has nice things to say."

"I'm afraid it is only Lizzie who has unkind words to say about me," Darcy added.

Fitz stopped in his tracks. "What exactly has my idiot cousin done to deserve that?" His smile was curious and friendly.

"I'm glad you asked; I've been wondering the same thing," Darcy replied drily.

"Well, how much time do you have before your party?" I responded.

"Oh, Darcy!" Fitz grabbed Darcy by the collar. "You have such a way with the ladies. Miss Bennet, on behalf of my family, my sincerest apologies for whatever offenses Sir Grumpsalot over here has bestowed upon you."

He reached out his hand and did a slight bow. I accepted

his hand with a laugh and nodded in acceptance of his kind gesture.

"Maybe I should skip the reunion and instead try to make amends. Come to think of it, there are a few former teachers that I wish to avoid." He winked at me.

Several girls from my dorm walked past with big, puffy garment bags.

"Oh, wow, I forgot that 'tis the season for prom insanity." Fitz shook his head. "Are you suffering from pre-prom pandemonium?"

"Absolutely not," I assured him.

"Good for you. Even some of Darcy's friends seem to have lost their minds. You had to talk one friend out of going with some real character, didn't you?"

Darcy's expression changed immediately.

I felt my blood begin to boil. I had assumed it was Caroline who was keeping Charles away from Jane. But it was Darcy. *Of course* it was Darcy.

"What's this?" I asked.

Darcy just brushed it away. "Nothing, it's nothing."

Yes, it was nothing to him. But it was *everything* to Jane.

"Oh!" Fitz glanced at his watch. "I must make my way to the

Headmaster's House. Lizzie, a pleasure." He shook my hand. "Cousin" — he turned to Darcy — "don't be an imbecile. Good families are dime-a-dozen, but a good woman is rare."

We watched him cross the quad toward Pemberley.

"I like him," I stated. Anybody who could give Darcy such a ribbing was all right in my book. I turned to head toward my dorm and was surprised when Darcy followed. "Is there something I can help you with?" I asked.

Darcy shook his head. "No, I just thought I'd walk you the rest of the way."

"Again, your concern for my well-being is so touching."

He replied with silence.

"So, how's Charles?"

He paused for a moment. "Charles is fine. He's been really busy."

"So I hear." I balled my fists up tightly. I even bit my tongue. Seeing Darcy on a regular basis was wearing my patience thin. And knowing that he was the cause of Jane's unhappiness made it almost unbearable.

"I work on Monday, Tuesday, and Friday nights, as well as Sunday afternoons," I said.

He stared at me.

I continued. "We seem to be running into each other a lot lately, and I thought you'd like to know my hours. So you can avoid them, of course."

He nodded abruptly, then turned away. I didn't expect to see him in the café again.

18.

ONCE AGAIN, I WAS WRONG. INSTEAD OF AVOIDING ME, DARCY was there at every shift. Sometimes he would leave when I was done and walk me back. I found it easier to not fight it. It was a short walk, and most of the time he would mercifully walk with me in silence. If we talked, it was generally small talk about classes.

"So where's your boyfriend?" Tara asked me one night.

"Who? Wick? He's not my boyfriend." As if I needed to be reminded.

"You know that's not who I'm talking about."

"Darcy?" I scoffed. "Please, he's more like a . . ."

"Stalker?"

I shook my head. "I believe stalkers have to generally care about their prey."

"Your bodyguard?"

"That would be ironic since he's the person I need protection from."

"Huh." Tara started to wipe down a counter.

"What?" I pried.

"You know what I find ironic?"

"No, but I have a feeling you're going to tell me."

She looked up at me. "That you complain about him, yet you always look when the door opens toward closing time, like you're waiting for him."

"No I don't."

I had to think about it. Did I?

"So why do you let him?" she asked.

"Well, he wears shoes and a shirt, so I can't really deny him service."

"You know that's not what I mean. Why do you let him walk you home?"

"I don't know. At first, I didn't want to put up a fight. I didn't think it would become a habit. But nobody really tries anything with me when he's around, and that's nice. I guess I've just gotten used to it."

The truth was: I could be myself on our walks. I didn't have to talk if I didn't want to. It wasn't like I had to pretend that everything in my life was great (like I have to with my parents). Or be on alert (like with the rest of my class). Or try to be supportive and upbeat (like with Jane).

With Darcy, I found that I could be me.

Occasionally, we'd talk about life back home. He'd ask me about my family or what I did over the weekend. But most of the time we walked in silence and it wasn't awkward. We had our own separate moments that we seemed to share in silence. It was natural, it wasn't forced, it was our own little routine.

Then, with two weeks until spring break, he broke the routine. Instead of letting me go off into my dorm without a good-bye of any sort, he took the moment of my departure to ask, "Can I speak to you?"

I shrugged. He'd had an opportunity to speak to me for the previous fifteen minutes, so I didn't see why now was any better a time. But he had a nervous look on his face, so curiosity got the best of me.

"Lizzie, Elizabeth . . . I don't think I can keep this up any longer. I like you. I like you a lot."

I was so astonished, I couldn't speak.

He continued. "I find myself thinking about you constantly —
against my better judgment, I might add. I keep trying to reason
with myself about why I'm so drawn to you. As much as I try, I
can't seem to talk myself out of it. You're like no one else I've
known . . . and that has nothing to do with your upbringing. I
mean, it's good and bad, I guess. Anyway, I would like to take
you to prom."

My initial instinct was to be polite, like with Colin. But I was
so offended and aggravated at his proposal that I was filled with
nothing but resentment.

"Despite what you might think of my *upbringing*," I began,
trying to control the anger in my voice, "I was raised to be
polite. I know I should thank you for your offer, but I won't.
The very last thing I want in this world is for you to think
anything of me, and there is no way I would ever go to prom
with you."

Darcy struggled to retain his composure. "Are you serious?
How could you say such a thing to me?"

"How could *I* say such things?" My voice was slowly rising.
"How could you even for a second think I would be thrilled to
hear that you like me *against your better judgment* . . . that you can't
talk yourself out of liking me? You are so full of yourself. You can't even

ask a girl to prom without insulting her, and you're too daft to even realize it!"

Darcy's face burned red. He opened up his mouth to speak, but I continued.

"And I have every reason to despise you. Are you so vain that you didn't realize this? You cost my best friend's happiness with Charles."

Darcy's eyes grew wide.

"Don't even try to deny it. I know it was you. You, who walks around with this holier-than-thou air about you, dictating who should be with who. Jane is the most wonderful person I have ever met. Yes, her father is in between jobs and her sister is brash, but who are you to tell Charles who he can and cannot date?

"And Wick! You couldn't contain your jealousy, could you? You couldn't stand the thought of a townie having the same connections as you. So what did you do? You got him expelled. You ruined his chance at a good education, of making something of himself. Honestly, it wouldn't surprise me if you tried to find some bogus reason to get me kicked out now that I've wounded your bloated pride. Although I sincerely doubt that anybody can do that to you. You selfish, spoiled jerk. I was liking it so much more when we were silent. When things weren't forced. Why did you have to speak?"

"You really believe this about me?" Darcy's voice was soft. "You certainly have made up your mind, haven't you?"

"Since the first moment I met you. You have been nothing but conceited and standoffish. I tried to make an effort for Jane's sake, but since that isn't an issue any longer, thanks to you, I don't have any reason to hide my feelings."

"No, no, you certainly aren't hiding anything." Darcy leaned against a tree. "Well, I've heard enough. I'm sorry for offending you with my proposal — that isn't what I intended to do. I'm . . ." He seemed lost for a moment. Then he stood up purposely and nodded at me. "Well, thanks for your time. Have a good night." He hurriedly walked toward Pemberley.

I rushed to my room, feeling outraged. I found a note from Jane on my computer screen, saying she was in the common room.

How could I have possibly attracted someone like Will Darcy? Not only that, but I had absolutely no idea that all this time he'd been flirting with me.

I fell to the floor, exhausted from everything — school, work, practice, and now this.

The dam finally burst. I had, once again, reached my breaking point.

I locked the door and broke down in tears.

19.

I DIDN'T HAVE THE STRENGTH TO TELL JANE WHAT HAPPENED. Not only could I not bear to repeat my conversation with Darcy, I didn't want to bring up my theory that Darcy was responsible for Charles's distance.

I decided to take a sick day that Monday and stayed in bed catching up on work. When I went to e-mail my Hoboken friends, I was shocked to find an e-mail from Darcy that he'd sent late the previous night.

Dear Lizzie,

Please know that I'm not stupid enough to make the same mistake twice. I'm not going to repeat myself here. But after thinking about what you said, I can understand why you have so much contempt for me. However, in fairness to us both, I think there are a few things you should know.

First, I want to apologize about how I treated you when we first met. I was rude to you at the party and, you were right, it was because you were a scholarship student. I spent the semester in London running away from some issues I had and it was really hard coming back. I think I might have taken it out on you. But then I got to know you and I was horrified by the assumptions that I had made about you. You are really an incredible person and I admire how brave you are (and I will admit you are the first person I've met at Pemberley or Longbourn who hasn't been impressed by my family's money, which made me like you even more). I hoped that your opinion of me would change if you gave me a second chance. I tried to figure out a way to make amends, but, obviously, it was all in vain. So if you take anything away from this letter, I hope it is that I am truly sorry for how I treated you.

Second, I am not directly responsible for what has happened with Charles and Jane. However, I am certainly at fault for not stepping in. I fully admit to that. I will also admit to being indirectly responsible. In fact, we both are. I believe the person responsible wanted to keep Jane away because this person also wanted to keep *you* away. As much as you were shocked by my revelation tonight, my feelings for you have been clear to those around me for quite some time. (I wanted to preface this all with "please don't think me conceited," but we both already know your feelings on that subject.) I should have straightened that situation out as well, and I have recently been inspired to clear the air with this person. Although I hope to spare her feelings more than mine were spared tonight. I plan to fix my errors, and while I know that Jane has been hurt, I hope that she can forgive Charles for being such an idiot.

I also wanted to clear up something my cousin said that I believe you misunderstood. The friend I talked out of going to the prom wasn't Charles. It was Colin. He was adamant about asking you again, but I convinced him otherwise. My selfish motives were clearly at play.

Lastly, the accusation that I got Wick kicked out of Pemberley because of my own jealousy couldn't be further from the truth. I don't like to speak about this, since it was a very painful time for my family, but I feel that I need to defend myself against whatever lies Wick may have told you.

George Wickham and I were good friends. We instantly clicked when we met, and we started spending a lot of time together. He was close with my whole family, including my fourteen-year-old sister, Georgiana. I always had him home on break, and my parents even gave him money for his school supplies and took him on vacation with us. I was happy that my father was going to help him with an internship at his law firm last summer. And, selfishly, I was happy to have him stay with us. He was like the brother I'd never had.

But Wick also liked to play as hard as he worked. Granted, I had a lot of fun hanging out with him, but he crossed the line when he got Georgie involved.

My sister means everything to me. You will never find a sweeter, more caring person. My parents were gone one weekend and I came home to find empty liquor bottles around the house. I walked in on Wick trying to take advantage of my sister, whom he had gotten drunk. Fortunately, I got home before anything else could've happened, but I will never forgive myself for putting my sister in that situation.

I kicked him out of our house, and my father withdrew his internship. But Wick knew our security codes and we, stupidly, didn't think to change them. He broke into our house and stole jewelry, cash, and some family items. We had the security footage to prove it.

That's why he got kicked out of Pemberley. In truth, he's lucky we didn't press charges for the robbery. We should have, but we didn't want to have to go through a trial and have it all come out in the press. He violated my trust, my family's trust, and, most reprehensible of all, he tried to take advantage of a young girl's innocent affections.

As you once reminded me, I did accuse you of having a problem with people with money. And I will admit to having a problem with people without it. But it was only because of Wick. I have never told anybody this, but what happened with Wick was the reason why I went to London last semester. I needed to get away from campus, and from the guilt I had about bringing someone like him into my family. So my guard was up when I returned to campus, and I wasn't ready to allow myself to be close to anybody new. It was very unfair of me to lump you in with someone like him, and again, for that I'm very sorry.

I don't expect this to really change anything between us. But I couldn't sleep without at least giving you my side of the story.

I truly do wish you the best with everything,

Will Darcy

I stared at the screen in a desperate attempt to comprehend everything Darcy had said. I reread his e-mail several times.

At first, I didn't believe anything — *couldn't* believe it. Then I thought some more about Jane and Charles. Even though Lydia had embarrassed Jane, it would make sense for Caroline to feel jealous about me when I was the only person Darcy had danced with the whole evening. The idea that Caroline knew Darcy's feelings for me seemed so surreal. So it was me she was trying to keep away, not Jane. I didn't know if I should have felt relieved or guilty about that.

I still kept reading the part about Wick. I thought: *Why should I believe Darcy?*

Then I reflected on Wick's behavior. Yes, he was charming and warm, but he never seemed interested in hanging out with me unless I was at work . . . and giving him free drinks.

And he *had* told me that we had to take advantage of our situation.

But this seemed so . . . extreme.

How well did I know Wick? And how well did I know Darcy?

I reread Darcy's last couple paragraphs and a knot formed in my stomach.

Darcy had a wall around him, just like me. But unlike me, Darcy's feelings had changed after he got to know me. He'd built some doors into the wall, while I'd held on to my prejudices the entire time.

Yes, he'd been cold to me when we first met, but ever since, he'd been making an attempt to get to know me, when I couldn't see past my own narrow-mindedness. He walked me home from work, he even tried to buy me a book, and all I did was be cold to him. He wasn't perfect. He would say the wrong things sometimes. But if he was a guy from Hoboken, I would have looked past it . . . or at least forgiven him. But since Darcy was rich, I couldn't.

I'd taken Wick at his word because he was a scholarship kid like me. But never once had I thought it was odd that he'd gotten kicked out of school without a proper explanation. Because I sympathized. Because I feared the same thing would happen to me. I'd assumed we were in the same boat, when really he was the shark swimming beneath it.

All this time I'd berated Darcy for his pride, but *I* was the one who'd been blinded by my own stubbornness.

What kind of person did that make me?

20.

I SPENT THE FOLLOWING WEEK IN A CONFUSED DAZE. IT WAS as if I was viewing my life through foggy lenses. I practically memorized Darcy's e-mail. I printed it out and kept it with my books, so I could pull it out and consult it if there was a word I'd forgotten, or a phrase that I wasn't completely sure of.

A swirl of conflicting emotions surfaced. One moment, I'd be furious at his prom invitation — his arrogance, his poor choice of words. Then I'd think about what his family had gone through because of Wick. But then I'd remember that he'd idly sat by and done nothing while Caroline had sabotaged Jane's relationship with Charles.

The worst was being at work. Anytime I heard the door open, I swung around, expecting to see him. But he never showed up.

I didn't know what I would've said to him if I'd seen him. I'd started to reply to his e-mail several times, but I didn't know what to say.

I thought it might be easier if he was actually in front of me. But I wouldn't blame him if he never wanted to speak to me again.

Friday night at the Java Junction was incredibly busy. Students were flocking in to get their caffeine fix to study for the following week's midterms.

I found myself almost desperate to see Darcy. I convinced myself that I would know what to do when I saw him. But as the hours ticked away, he was nowhere to be found.

To make matters worse, I had two surprising visitors.

Lydia . . . with Wick.

Lydia practically skipped to the counter, Wick only a few paces away. "Hey, Lizzie," she said, "get me the usual and whatever he wants."

I hadn't seen Wick since receiving Darcy's e-mail. I concentrated on making their drinks and replayed in my head everything

Darcy had written. Then I revisited my conversations with Wick. There was a part of me that knew something wasn't adding up right.

"Here you go," I said, handing them their order and ringing it up.

Lydia was clawing through the chocolate snacks near the register. "I don't even want to deal with my exams, ya know? I mean, like, how can anybody concentrate when the weather is getting better? And I'm, like, so ready for break. Even though we're going to be stuck in the city. Hey!" She grabbed Wick's arm. "You should totally come visit me in New York. I'm so going to need you to save me."

Wick raised his eyebrow at me, and for a brief moment I smiled. Despite my better judgment.

"What are you doing for the break?" he asked me.

"I'm going to be home with my parents."

Lydia, bored by the conversation, went over to add even more sugar to her chocolate drink.

"I'll be sure to let you know if I'm in the city."

I didn't respond.

"You know, I tried to stop by here the last couple of weeks, but a certain person was always here."

"You mean Will?"

"Ick." Lydia scrunched her face up in disgust. "That guy is, like, always so serious. What's his problem?"

Wick laughed. "Where do you want us to start? Right, Lizzie?"

I paused for a moment before asking, "Did you know his parents' house was robbed last year?"

I studied Wick's reaction. His face held still, but it seemed like it was forced, as if he had to control himself from revealing something. The truth, perhaps.

"So, you two are becoming close?" he finally replied.

I shrugged. "Not really. We've just been talking. It's been . . . illuminating."

"I'm sure it has." He turned to Lydia. "Let's get out of here."

Lydia grabbed Wick's arm and started heading toward the door.

"Uh, Lydia, can you give Jane a message for me?" I called out to her.

Wick remained at the door while Lydia approached the counter. "Can't you just call her?"

"My cell phone is broken," I lied.

"Not surprising. That thing is, like, so old."

Lydia looked at me with bored eyes, so I plunged right in. "Um, why are you hanging out with Wick?" I whispered.

"I called him."

"How did you get his number?"

"The day you introduced me. I've been talking to him, and then when I found out he's single again —"

"What?"

"Yeah." Lydia played with her straw and started looking around. Her attention span was sporadic at best. "I don't know, he dumped Sylvia, whatever. He could never have feelings for someone as vile as her."

"I think you should be careful — he's three years older than you."

"I know, right? How cool is that?"

"Lydia . . ."

"Do you have a message for Jane or not?"

"No, it's okay. I'll use the phone in the back."

Once Lydia and Wick were gone, I called Jane from my perfectly fine (and only two years old) cell phone and left a message. As soon as my shift was over, I hurried to our room and found her waiting for me at her desk.

I let it all out. I told her everything — Caroline's interference, Darcy's proposal, the things I said to him, his e-mail. I didn't tell her exactly what had happened with Wick. I assumed it wasn't my place to give out those horrific details.

After a few moments in silence, absorbing everything, Jane came over and sat down next to me.

"I had no idea, Lizzie," she said. "I thought you were just really stressed from exams."

"I'm sorry — I should have told you about Charles before, but I didn't know if it was going to make you feel any better."

She sighed. "There's really nothing I can do about Charles. I guess I shouldn't be surprised about Caroline's behavior. She's so manipulative and has always liked bossing Charles around. I've always been nice to her, even though she is a total snob. I'll still be nice, but we're not friends."

"Jane, that is the worst thing I've ever heard you say about somebody else. Nicely done!"

Jane tried to smile, but she looked tired. "I have to do something about Lydia. I talked to my mom about it, and she just said that Lydia's going through her wild stage. To be honest, I think my parents are happy to have some peace and quiet in the house with her gone."

"Lucky them."

Jane drifted off then, at least for a moment. It wasn't hard to imagine what she was thinking about.

"What are you going to do about Charles?" I asked. "I mean, now that you know."

She shrugged.

"Nothing," she told me. "Regardless of his sister's interference, this is his doing, his mistake. If he doesn't see that, he really isn't worth it in the first place."

I nodded in agreement.

While Jane seemed strong, I could sense that she was still hurt. The lies, the fighting, the manipulation . . . it was all so tiring. But there were still some things worth fighting for.

And Jane's happiness was one of them.

21.

*J*ANE TRIED TO KEEP A TIGHT LEASH ON LYDIA THAT WEEKEND.
Lydia kept slipping out and wouldn't answer her phone.

Saturday evening, Jane and I decided to take a walk around campus to clear our heads.

"I have this huge desire to out Wick for the opportunistic gold digger he is," I admitted.

"I would have to agree with you, but I'm not sure that's what Darcy would want."

Yes, there was Darcy to consider.

Darcy, who'd gone missing this past week.

Darcy, who I'd been thinking about a lot lately.

"I know it isn't any of my business, but . . . and I can't believe I'm about ready to say this, but I think Darcy has gotten a bad rap."

Jane burst out laughing. "Lizzie! The only person who has really given him grief is YOU. Everybody here already knew him. He can be pretty serious, yes, but he's a great guy. I can't be sure, but I bet I've told you this a million times before."

I didn't want to be reminded of what a close-minded person I'd been. I kept trying to reconcile everything in my mind.

We started to climb up the steep hill toward our dorm. The sun was setting and the lights outside the large residence hall had been turned on. Someone was silhouetted beneath one of the lights.

As we got closer, we realized it was Charles, holding a bouquet of roses.

Jane stopped short as Charles turned around. His face beamed when he saw her.

"Lizzie . . ." she said softly to me.

Charles approached us slowly.

"Jane, would it be okay if I talked to you alone?" he asked apprehensively.

I smiled at them both and started heading inside.

"No, wait," Jane called out after me. "There isn't anything you can say to me that you can't say in front of Lizzie."

I stood awkwardly next to them. It seemed that Jane wanted to make this as uncomfortable as possible for Charles. I couldn't blame her.

Charles gently grabbed Jane's hand. "I'm so sorry for everything, Jane. I truly am. I have been distant, cold, a total fool. I'm an idiot. A complete and total idiot."

"Charles . . ." Jane blushed slightly.

"The entire semester in London, all I could think of was you. I couldn't wait to get back here and see you. And what do I do? I completely mess everything up. I know you have such a kind heart, Jane. That is the only reason I have an ounce of hope that you can forgive me."

Jane looked down at the ground. I could tell that she was fighting back tears.

Charles leaned in closer to her. "There's no point in me going to prom, unless it's with you. There's no point in me doing anything, unless it's with you."

Jane lifted her head up and let Charles see the tear trickling down her face. "Of course I forgive you."

I quietly walked away, not wanting to intrude any further on their moment.

As I headed back inside, I started to think about Darcy and what he'd said. In his e-mail he'd said he was going to fix things between Charles and Jane. It seemed as if he had.

Later that night, I saw Caroline with bloodshot eyes. It seemed as if he may have corrected her as well.

Darcy was starting to put everything back together.

So much so, that Jane's trip to Vera for a prom dress was not in vain.

22.

I MAY HAVE BEEN WRONG ABOUT WICK AND DARCY, BUT I had always known that Charles Bingley was wonderful. And I was so happy to be right about someone (for once). His connections had almost cut off his connection, but in the end, the truest connection had prevailed.

A dark cloud had lifted. The week of midterms was pretty uneventful, and that was a good thing. All of my exams went well. Jane was happy. It looked like I was going to be able to keep my scholarship.

Unfortunately, not all was going smoothly. I was having trouble with my recital piece.

"Try it again, but slower," Mrs. Gardiner said to me after I botched a complicated run for the third time.

I closed my eyes for a second and took a deep breath. I lightly ran my fingers over the keys, trying to get my brain and fingers to work together to go through the most difficult sequence in Rhapsody. I slowed the pace and was able to hit every note.

"Perfect. Now faster."

I went up to tempo and my fingers ran into each other. A horrible sound erupted from the piano.

"Sorry, I've been practicing, really. I'll work on it over break."

Mrs. Gardiner smiled at me. "I know you will. But I have another assignment for you over the break."

I held in a groan. Rhapsody was challenging enough.

Mrs. Gardiner went over to her desk and pulled out an envelope. "You know Claudia Reynolds?"

"Of course!"

Claudia Reynolds was my idol. Any time I got stuck on a piece, I'd find footage of her playing it to try to figure it out. The emotion she put into her music was without equal, and her phrasing was always perfect.

"Well, this is for you." She handed me an envelope, and inside were two tickets to see Claudia Reynolds that weekend at Carnegie Hall.

I was stunned. "I can't . . ."

Mrs. Gardiner waved my protest away. "Nonsense. It's my pleasure. You deserve it."

I thanked her profusely and immediately called my mother to tell her our plans for Saturday afternoon. Having that to look forward to made the remainder of the week, including the rest of my exams, bearable.

I could hardly wait to get back home. Every time I returned to the city Jane offered me a ride with her and Lydia. But, as always, I declined and took the ninety-minute train ride from town to Grand Central Station. No other Longbourn or Pemberley student would be caught dead on mass transit, so I knew I would be alone. I needed the solitude before going home, a chance to detox myself from all the negativity and pressure of campus. It was as if I dropped off my emotional baggage at each station stop along the way.

By the time the train arrived in Manhattan and I saw my parents and a couple friends waiting for me at the kiosk in the middle of the station, I was the old Lizzie. The happy, warm Lizzie of yesteryear. They embraced me and instantly I knew that despite the remaining commute back to Hoboken, I was already home.

23.

BEING HOME, SLEEPING IN MY OWN BED, HANGING OUT with my old friends, gave me the centering I needed after the past few confusing weeks.

Even though I'd spoken on the phone with my parents every weekend, they acted as if they knew nothing of the past two and a half months. Over Saturday morning breakfast, they grilled me about classes, friends (they were under the impression that I had more than just two friends, and I didn't want to correct, or worry, them), the recital, and even the dreaded P-word.

"Isn't prom a big deal at Longbourn?" Mom asked. "I remember it from that brochure we had."

I shrugged. "Not really." I envisioned the majority of my classmates experiencing an unexpected shiver down their spine at my blatant lie.

"Do you want to look at dresses while we are in the city today?"

"No, that's okay."

Mom came over and hugged me. "I'm so glad you're home. I don't like you being so far away. This house is entirely too quiet without you and although I know how hard you're working, I plan on you playing that piano while you are here. I just had it tuned!"

Our piano was from my father's childhood, complete with ivory keys. It had family history, but it wasn't the greatest-sounding instrument. After playing the gorgeous grand pianos at school, it was always a shock to my system to play the upright. But it was what I grew up on, and I loved it regardless. It had character, and I had learned many times this past year that money does not buy character.

In the early afternoon, Mom and I headed into the city for the concert. I had butterflies in my stomach. I always walked by Carnegie Hall when I was in the city. That was the dream — to play there. In the meantime, I would settle for this. Not only did I get to go to Carnegie Hall, but I was going to see one of my favorite pianists. I was still touched by Mrs. Gardiner's kindness — this was her way of suggesting that my own break wasn't that far away. Which made going to Longbourn seem strangely worth it.

My pulse began to quicken as we approached the building. As we entered the main hall, my breath was nearly knocked out of me. The chairs on the stage were dwarfed by the high ceiling and ornate columns on the sides. I turned around and saw the balcony seating, which seemed to reach the sky. I looked up and could practically feel the glow from the oval set of lights that illuminated the hall.

An usher escorted us to our seats, which were in the fourth row on the aisle. I could see the keyboard on the grand piano that was commanding center stage.

"My goodness, Lizzie," Mom remarked. "You must be the perfect student in order to get such royal treatment."

I smiled. I was happy I could do this for my mom. She was the reason that I had first gotten into music. She loved it, but couldn't play. She tried but didn't seem to have the capacity for it. And since, at least according to her, I began banging on the piano when I was old enough to walk to the upright, she enrolled me in lessons by the time I was four.

When I'd run out of teachers in the Hoboken area who could challenge me, she'd started taking me into the city. She'd spent so much money on my lessons, I didn't want to disappoint her.

Music was our thing. We'd listen to albums together, I'd put on concerts just for her. And now I was able to take my mother to Carnegie Hall.

"Someday, Elizabeth, someday," she said to me as she squeezed my hands.

The lights went down and the orchestra members took their places, followed by the conductor. The spotlight lit up and Claudia Reynolds, beautiful in a black floor-length strapless dress, her hair up in a twist, approached the piano to an ovation from both the orchestra and the audience.

She graciously bowed before sitting down at the piano.

The orchestra started playing Mozart's Piano Concerto no. 24, K.491. The strings came in, followed by the wind instruments. As the music began to take over the space, I leaned forward in my seat, anticipating Reynolds's first notes at the piano. The piano melody, at first so simple, was beautiful. I could see Reynolds's eyes closed, her body swaying back and forth, her embrace of the music.

I closed my eyes and let the music take over. I felt moisture in my eyes from being overwhelmed by the setting, the music, the performer.

It was flawless. It was, in fact, so flawless that it didn't call attention to its own flawlessness. It was perfect.

The next piece was Chopin's Piano Concerto no. 2. Again, she took the entire audience of almost three thousand people on an emotional journey. I found, not surprisingly, that I had a smile on my face the entire time. Carnegie Hall was my equivalent of a candy store and I was on a sugar high.

After Chopin, there was an intermission. I was in awe of the entire performance. But when I looked and saw what was next, Rachmaninoff's Piano Concerto no. 3, I was stunned. That was one of the most challenging piano solos and very different in tone from the previous two pieces.

We returned to our seats after the intermission and I was alarmed when I saw an usher waiting for us. "Miss Bennet?" he said as my mother and I approached our seats.

"Yes?" I had a feeling this was too good to be true. That my fairy tale of an afternoon was coming to an end and that we would be marked as frauds. You could take the girl out of Longbourn, but apparently not the sense of uncertainty.

"This note is for you." He handed me an envelope with my name scrawled on it. I opened it and found a letter inside that was on heavy, expensive, cream stock. I gasped when I saw CLAUDIA REYNOLDS engraved on the top with her address.

Dear Elizabeth,

*I'm so happy you were able to come to the performance today.
I've heard so much about you and I'd be honored if you and your
guest would join me for high tea at my house following the concert.*

Yours truly,
Claudia Reynolds

"Oh, my," Mom said as she read over my shoulder. "How on
earth does she know who you are?"

"Mrs. Gardiner, I guess. I knew she had connections, but I
can't believe she would do this for me." I sank down in my plush
seat. Claudia Reynolds knew who I was, and was inviting me to
her house.

"Can we go, please? I know we have dinner plans with Dad."
My voice was near hysterics.

"Your father can starve as far as I'm concerned." Mom
winked at me.

When Claudia Reynolds returned to the stage, I was even more
mesmerized by her performance. The concentration she had while
approaching the near-impossible runs was astonishing. I tried to
keep track of her fingers, but they were flying. I wanted to absorb
everything about her performance, to try to walk away with some

understanding of how I was going to pull off the less difficult, but still challenging, Rhapsody.

When the last note faded, she received a well-deserved standing ovation.

I was in complete and utter awe. One of my idols was standing before me, after performing the most wonderful concert I had ever had the pleasure of attending. And she was inviting me to her house.

Thinking back on all the torture that I had endured at Longbourn, I knew at that moment that it had been worth it. That I could have more days with nasty taunts, but at the end of the day, I was a student that Mrs. Gardiner respected enough to give me this amazing moment. I may not have had the respect of many of the students, but they didn't matter. I was never going to earn any respect from the snobs, but to people who could see past such inconsequential things as money and status, I had the potential to be someone special.

Maybe I would even be one of the few who would get to experience what Claudia Reynolds was experiencing at that very moment. Standing center stage, being lauded for her talent — because that was what should truly matter in this world. What you have to offer people, not what you can buy.

After the concert, Mom and I walked slowly along Central Park to Claudia Reynolds's brownstone, which overlooked the park. My mind was spinning with what I was going to say to her — if I could even get anything out. I was still shocked by her invitation and felt a panic come over me as we approached the address on the card. My pulse was racing and my palms were sweating as we ascended the steps to the front door.

The biggest shock of the day, however, didn't turn out to be the invitation. There were many people I anticipated to see when the door opened — servants, maids, Claudia Reynolds herself — but the person who greeted us was the last person on earth I expected.

Will Darcy.

24.

I STARED BACK AND FORTH BETWEEN THE NUMBER ON THE side of the brownstone and the invitation in my hand, trying to see how I could've gotten the address horribly wrong.

"Mrs. Bennet?" Darcy smiled warmly at my mother. "It's so nice to meet you. I'm Will, Claudia's son."

My heart stopped. *Will Darcy is Claudia Reynolds's son?*

My mother shook Darcy's hand as she entered their main foyer. "Hi, Lizzie. Nice to see you," Darcy greeted me.

Mom was surprised. "Do you two know each other?"

"I go to Pemberley, Mrs. Bennet."

Before Mom could say anything, Claudia Reynolds rushed to greet us. "Hello, Elizabeth! Mrs. Bennet! Welcome!"

She hugged me and kissed me on both cheeks. "Oh, Elizabeth, I have heard so much about you and your playing. And you must be Elizabeth's mother!"

"Please, call me Judy."

I couldn't find my voice. I was stunned into absolute silence.

Ms. Reynolds . . . Mrs. Darcy . . . *Darcy's mom* . . . welcomed us into the living room where a tower of scones, finger sandwiches, brownies, and cookies was waiting for us. While my mother asked about a painting that hung over the fireplace, Darcy leaned in.

"I can't tell if you're mad or surprised," he whispered.

"I'm shocked."

He smiled at me. "Elizabeth Bennet, could it possibly be that you're speechless?" He nudged me playfully.

I looked at him, *truly* looked at him for the first time in what felt like a long time. I noticed that there was something different about him. He was dressed in worn jeans and a T-shirt, his hair slightly messy. He seemed . . . relaxed.

"Your mom . . ." I tried to get out.

"Yes, I'm sorry. I didn't think you'd take the tickets if you knew they were from me. The invitation here was my mom's idea.

I couldn't bear to let her know —" He stopped abruptly. "I guess I didn't want her to know your opinion of me."

"Why didn't you . . . the e-mail . . . I tried to reply, I just . . . I'm so sorry, I . . ." I couldn't form a single thought. So much was racing through my mind. "Thank you for talking to Charles."

"It was the right thing to do. I should have done it sooner."

"Shall we?" Ms. Reynolds gestured for us to sit down. I looked around the living room and couldn't believe how comfortable it was. There were overstuffed couches and a chaise longue surrounding a glass coffee table. It was obvious everything was high-end, but it didn't scream pretentious or expensive, even though I was pretty sure the painting my mom was asking about was an original Pollock.

"Lizzie?" Mom prompted me. Apparently, Darcy wasn't the only one surprised by my silence.

I looked up and saw Claudia Reynolds smiling at me.

"Ms. Reynolds." I tried to find my voice. "I cannot tell you enough how much meeting you means to me. You are truly amazing. The concert was, and will forever be, one of the most incredible experiences of my life. Thank you." I bit my lip to stop it from quivering.

She smiled at me. "Thank you, Lizzie. Can I call you Lizzie?"

I nodded. She could pretty much call me anything. I wouldn't even be offended if Claudia Reynolds called me a charity case, bum, or hobo.

"So, please, help yourself." She gestured toward the food in front of us. "Will, can you pour the tea, please? I would like to take credit for this, but our amazing cook is from England and makes the best scones and clotted cream. We only have it for special guests or the cream wouldn't be the only thing that is clotted in this house."

Darcy groaned. "You're never going to get tired of that joke, are you?"

"Never," she said as she grabbed a scone.

"Georgiana, there you are!" She got up and gave the girl who entered the room a big hug.

Darcy's sister gave us a little wave as she was introduced to us before sitting down next to her brother. She was so tiny and frail, I felt sick to my stomach thinking about Wick.

Darcy grabbed a plate and started filling it up for her. The admiration between the two was obvious. "Hmmm," he started teasing her. "Which one of these cups is for you? I don't see any black licorice tea here."

"Gross, Will," she said softly as she pushed his arm.

"Lizzie, do you see any ant stew near you for Georgie?"

"Will, stop it! I'm not five years old anymore." She giggled, and it was clear that she didn't mind being teased by her older brother.

"Okay, fine, have it your way. The adults will be drinking tea, but here you go." He picked up a cup of hot chocolate with whipped cream. "I don't know. Looks pretty gross to me, but whatever."

She took the cup and sat back on the couch, her feet barely grazing the floor. She was the same age as Lydia, but unlike Lydia (well, there was a lot about Georgiana that was different from Lydia), she didn't try to come across as older. She seemed a lot younger, more vulnerable. I noticed throughout the evening that she kept studying me, although it was a very different look than the judging glances I would get from Caroline. Georgiana was more curious. I wondered what, if anything, Darcy had told her about me.

The thought of my treatment toward Darcy made me feel incredibly guilty during the tea, especially since his family was so warm and welcoming.

I hardly spoke, just observed, and kept trying to put all the pieces of this puzzle together.

Ms. Reynolds turned her attention to me. "So, Lizzie, what are you performing for the year-end recital?"

"Rhapsody on a Theme of Paganini."

"Impressive," she replied. "I didn't tackle that until I went to college. I'd love to hear you play." She nodded to the Steinway that was near the front window.

"Oh, well, I'm having some problems with the runs."

She nodded knowingly. "The last variation?"

"Yes."

"That's a tough one. The sheet music that I learned it on had the most ridiculous fingering recommendations. I guess it could be considered helpful, if you have six-fingered hands. Here, I'll show you a trick." She got up and motioned for me to join her at the piano.

I was in a near trance as I walked over to the bench.

"What I figured out is that if you cross over at this point" — she played part of the run — "it lets your fingers easily move up." She did it once slowly so I could see, and then again at full speed.

She got up so I could try. I tried to not be too intimidated as she stood behind me and I tried her method. It worked. It worked so well that for the first time I was able to do the entire run without my fingers running into themselves.

"Thank you!" I hesitated for a second and then did it again to make sure it wasn't a fluke.

"May we hear what you have so far? That's one of my favorite pieces."

Claudia Reynolds was asking me to play for her. Claudia Reynolds, who had just performed at Carnegie Hall. Claudia Reynolds, who had just taught me how to do a flawless run.

Claudia Reynolds, who was Will Darcy's mother.

The only thing that made sense to me was Rachmaninoff.

I gently ran my fingers over the keyboard, going over the piece in my mind. Then I began. I hadn't played the piece for anybody except Mrs. Gardiner. I generally got nervous performing new pieces for people. I would always start with my mom, then my dad, then my friends. But this time I dove in headfirst.

I don't even know if I breathed for the entire piece. I completely expected to forget a section or stumble, but I didn't. I hadn't even played all the different variations back-to-back yet, but there I was, in Claudia Reynolds's house . . . in Darcy's house, playing.

When I finished, I looked up and was somewhat startled to find Darcy standing right next to the piano with Georgiana.

I blushed, embarrassed that I would be seen as showing off.

The group applauded and I saw that my mother had tears running down her face. "I'm so proud of you," she sobbed.

Darcy's mom came over and gave me a hug. "That was brilliant."

"Because of you. I can't thank you enough for everything, really," I blubbered.

"Will and Georgiana, do either of you play?" Mom asked.

Will shook his head. "I tried, but I wasn't that good at it. I apparently didn't inherit the musical genius gene. But Georgie, on the other hand." Georgiana's face reddened. "She can sing and play both the piano and the flute."

"I'd love to hear you," I said.

She replied softly, "I'll play the flute," and then went running upstairs.

"Wow." Darcy looked at his mom.

Ms. Reynolds was beaming. "She must really like you; she generally won't play for new people."

Georgie came down and treated us to a mini-concert of a few Mozart and Bach solos. Her cheeks were ruddy from the attention, but she was magnificent. I caught glimpses of Darcy watching. He was clearly proud of her. I couldn't imagine what it must have been like for him to have one of his supposed closest friends try to take advantage of her.

After Georgie's concert and kind words from the group, Ms. Reynolds gave us a tour. "I'm so sorry Will Senior couldn't be here today. He's traveling on business. We made a pact that at least one of us had to be home at all times."

Their house was large, and not just by Manhattan standards. It was five stories, complete with a screening room, library, music room, billiards room, and a rooftop pool. It wasn't ostentatious, it was roomy and comfortable. Exactly the opposite of what I would have pictured Darcy's home to be like.

The place was filled with pictures of the four of them on vacation. There was a particularly embarrassing one of Darcy on a sailboat when he was twelve.

"Oh, wow," I said as I took in a photo of a young sunburned Darcy with metal braces and a baseball hat with droopy dog ears holding a fishing rod with a very tiny fish attached at the hook. "Don't they make clear braces? I thought metal ones were just for charity cases."

"Yes, well, I was told it would build character. Apparently not. As I'm sure you can imagine, this is my least-favorite part of the tour." We both laughed, and it startled me how friendly we were both being. That it didn't feel forced. Like during our walks . . . before he decided to talk.

I smiled at him. The reason it wasn't forced was because I was being normal. I'd found the door in his wall, and was just now opening mine. I had so much to say to him, so much to apologize for.

I kept thinking back on everything that I had said about him, all those horrible things I'd thought. And here he surprised me by giving me tickets to see his mom and opened his house to us. I didn't know what I did to deserve such thoughtful treatment from someone whom I had so openly loathed.

While our mothers were discussing having their children away at school, Darcy motioned for me to join him on the roof. The view of the park and east side of Manhattan was amazing.

"So, I have a favor to ask you," he said to me.

Immediately, the prom sprang to mind. He was going to ask me again, but this time, I wasn't sure what my answer would be.

He nervously drummed his fingers against the banister. "Georgie really seems to like you — I guess it's a Darcy trait. She wants to come visit you in Hoboken, since she's never been, if that would be all right with you." He looked down at the street.

"Of course."

He turned his back on the view and looked at me. "I guess I should have told you who my mother was."

I shook my head. "It's okay, I don't know . . ." I stopped myself from finishing that sentence. What I was going to say was I didn't know if that would've made a difference. If I'd liked Darcy solely because of his mother, I wouldn't have been any different from the snobs at Longbourn who didn't like me because my parents weren't famous, or rich, or from a "proper upbringing."

"Yes, well." He clearly was aware of what I was going to say. "To be honest, you're probably the only person who would have cared. My father's law practice seems to be what most people want to . . ." This time he was the one to stop himself.

"I'm really sorry about that," I offered.

"Well . . ." His voice trailed off into the night.

"And I'm sorry that I didn't respond to your e-mail. I tried to, but I guess I didn't know what to say. I'm not entirely proud of my behavior. And I . . ." Something hit me, and I felt like an idiot for not figuring it out before. I looked at Will. "You gave me the coat." It wasn't a question. It was a revelation. "Why didn't you say anything?"

"Would you have kept it if I had?"

I felt like the worst person on earth. "I . . ."

He looked out at the park. "I didn't want to believe what you said about how you were treated at Longbourn. But after our conversation in the bookstore, I started paying attention. It seems ridiculous that it wasn't something that I'd noticed before. I'd genuinely thought Cat accidentally spilled her coffee on you. I guess it's easy to ignore something you don't have to experience. And when I truly looked, I was so horrified to see what you went through. And when your coat was stolen . . . well, I wanted to do something to help, but knew you wouldn't accept it."

"How can you be so thoughtful to someone who has been so unkind?"

Will opened his mouth to speak, but we were interrupted.

"Will?" Georgiana came out onto the roof. "Did you ask?" she said meekly as she leaned against his arm.

He nodded. Georgiana looked like she was going to explode from happiness.

"Can we come tomorrow?" she asked.

"Georgie . . ." Darcy elbowed her gently. "Be polite."

"No, it's fine," I said. "Tomorrow works. You know what? You should take the ferry over. It's really pretty although it's . . . actually, nothing. The ferry would be fun."

I almost mentioned that the ferry was nearly four times more expensive than the train or bus to Hoboken, but realized that it probably wouldn't be an issue for them.

After we figured out our plans for the next day, we said our good-byes. I still had trouble speaking to his mother, *Claudia Reynolds*, and tried my best to not completely gush again at her brilliance.

As Mom and I headed to Port Authority to get the bus home, she grabbed my hand, like she used to do when I was little and we were visiting Manhattan.

"Elizabeth, that was such an amazing evening. That Will is charming and very handsome. Why haven't you mentioned him before?"

I tried to not laugh as I certainly *had* mentioned Will several times to my mother, but never by his proper name. Instead she'd heard the many names I'd given him, like "vile human being" and "pompous jerk."

Now I lied. "I didn't really know him that well — at least, not as well as I do now."

It was only later, as I sat with that thought, that I realized that it wasn't really a lie, after all. It was the absolute truth.

25.

I WAS EXTREMELY ANXIOUS THE NEXT DAY AS I WATCHED THE ferry carrying Darcy and Georgiana dock at the 14th Street pier in Hoboken.

Our greeting was a little awkward. I received a big hug from Georgiana, but when Darcy and I looked at each other, it wasn't clear whether we should shake hands, hug, or something else. So we simply nodded at each other. I'm pretty sure I heard Georgie sigh under her breath.

I took them on a walking tour of Hoboken. We headed along the waterfront and viewed the Manhattan skyline.

Georgie took out her phone. "I want to take a picture of you two." She held up her phone and motioned for us to get together.

Darcy and I lined up against the railing. "No, I need you closer together to get you both in the photo," she instructed.

I had taken countless pictures on the waterfront and I knew that if you were getting the skyline in the background, you didn't need to be *that* close.

Darcy put his arm around my shoulder and we leaned in. I slipped my arm around his waist and noticed how easily I fit into the little nook in his side.

"Oh, hold on, I'm having problems." Georgie played with her phone for a few moments while we just stood there in our posed embrace.

"Georgie . . ."

She looked up at her brother and blushed. "Um, I think it works now."

I felt Darcy's body begin shaking slightly and looked up to discover he was laughing. He leaned in and whispered, "She's very well meaning, if not subtle."

My cheeks began to burn from the embarrassment. I decided to distract them (and myself) by talking endlessly about the history of Hoboken — Frank Sinatra, *On the Waterfront*, anything that sprang in my mind while we walked around.

We grabbed sandwiches at Vito's Deli and cupcakes at Sweet, then grabbed a picnic bench in Church Square Park. Georgie grilled me relentlessly about my music history, where I practiced, where I want to go to college.

I turned the tables on her and brought up her own classes and music. "Why aren't you at Longbourn?" I asked.

Her face fell. "I want to stay closer to home."

I was horrified that I might have brought up a painful subject. It wouldn't be surprising that she didn't want to go to Longbourn, especially since Wick was a local.

"Oh, well, there's one person here who hasn't gotten a grilling yet." I tried to salvage the conversation by turning the attention to Darcy. "Are you prepared for the third degree?" I challenged him.

"I'll tell you whatever you want to know," Georgie offered.

"Fabulous," Darcy deadpanned.

"Okay, okay." There was so much that I wanted to know but was too afraid to ask, especially in front of him. "Most embarrassing Will moment."

Darcy groaned while Georgie clapped her hands. "That one's so easy!"

"Don't you dare," he warned her. "The river is close by and I would have no problem throwing you in."

She studied him for a moment. "I can swim," she stated, then turned to me. "Will used to have the greatest voice. He would sing in all these choirs and have solos."

Darcy put his head on the picnic table.

"Then one day," she continued, "his voice started changing in the middle of a solo during a Christmas recital at Lincoln Center."

"*You* sang at Lincoln Center?"

Darcy looked up from the table. "I don't think you could really call what I did singing."

Georgie was giggling. "It was so awful. He just kept trying to sing and then a huge squeak would come out."

"Okay, thank you." He swatted at her. "Now you have to say something nice about me to make up for that."

Georgie didn't even hesitate. "He's the best brother in the world. He's always been there for me. Always. And . . ." She looked at the ground.

A knowing silence fell over the table. It was only broken by my cell phone's ringtone. I apologized while I reached for it and saw it was Jane. I walked away from the table as I picked up.

"Lizzie?" I could instantly tell from the sound of her voice that something was wrong. "I don't know what to do. I need your help."

"Of course. What is it?"

Her voice was winded. "I can't find Lydia. She left a few hours ago, and the one time she picked up the phone she said she was with Wick and that she was sick of being treated like a child and was going to have some real fun. I have a really bad feeling about this. She isn't answering her phone. I know you said he can't be trusted, and I'm really worried about her."

I'd never given Jane the full details of what Wick was capable of, and I started cursing myself for not having been firmer about Lydia's obsession with Wick.

"I'm heading into the city now. Just keep trying her and tell her that she can*not* trust him."

I turned around and was startled that Darcy was right in front of me. "Is everything okay?"

I glanced over at Georgie and kept my voice down. "No, things are not okay. It's Jane's sister, Lydia. She's gone missing . . . with Wick."

Darcy instantly tensed at the sound of his name. He clenched his jaw and straightened up his back. The calm, relaxed manner was gone, and the Darcy that I first met seemed to be back.

"This is all my fault," I said.

"Your fault?" Darcy pulled out his cell phone. "No, this isn't your fault. It's my fault."

"But if it wasn't for me, Lydia would've never met him."

Darcy's voice was very controlled, almost too controlled. "No, we should have put him away. . . ." He glanced over at Georgie.

"I have to go into the city. I don't really know what I can do, but I really need to be there for Jane."

He nodded. "Let me talk to Georgie. I want to help you."

"You really don't —"

He cut me off. "Don't be silly."

Darcy leaned down to his sister and whispered something into her ear. I didn't know what he said at the time, but she responded in a positive way. So I had to assume she had no idea Wick was involved.

We quickly walked to the train station, and the short ride into the city felt like an eternity. I wasn't a good enough actress to pretend that I wasn't nervous, so I kept asking Georgie questions so I wouldn't be forced to lie about anything.

When the train pulled up to the first stop at Christopher Street, we all got out. Darcy flagged down a taxi and put Georgie into it. "Have fun!" she exclaimed as the cab pulled away.

"What exactly did you tell her we were doing?" I asked.

Darcy hesitated. "I don't think you will be happy to hear this, but I figured the only thing I could think of that wouldn't have made her want to come along or get her suspicious was to tell her that we were going on a date." He flagged down another cab and we got inside.

As we headed toward Jane's family's apartment in Tribeca, I studied him. He was so tense. I could tell that anger was bubbling up inside of him.

"I'm so sorry," I said. "Darcy, I'm so sorry that I've brought him into your life again. I didn't know. . . ."

He stared straight ahead. "How could you know? I should have done something. It isn't your fault."

"But I believed him. I thought he was like me. I was so stubborn and thought that we were similar, with the whole scholarship thing."

Darcy handed the taxi driver the fare as we arrived at Jane's. Before he got out, he looked at me.

"Lizzie," he said, "you are nothing like George Wickham."

26.

JANE WAS IN HYSTERICS WHEN SHE OPENED THE DOOR. BUT IT didn't take her that long to realize that I came with a guest. "Darcy?" she said in between sobs, glancing between the two of us.

Darcy took over, asking Jane where Lydia was last, what she had said, where she liked to hang out. Then he did probably the hardest thing — he told Jane the truth about Wick.

I looked down at the floor when he recounted the story he had e-mailed me. He kept control of his voice, but the one time I dared to look up, his hands were balled up in fists.

"I'm sorry that I didn't tell you this sooner," he said to Jane. "But the only reason I'm telling you this now is not to make you feel worse, but for you to understand what we have to do next."

Jane and I were both confused.

"We have to call around to hotels to see if they checked in anywhere."

"What?" Jane exclaimed. "She's fourteen years old!"

"Does she have a credit card?"

"Of course."

He studied me for a second. "Lizzie, I need you to start calling hotels."

"Like the Waldorf?" I had never stayed at a hotel in the city in my life. There were thousands of hotels, and I had no idea where to start.

"No, Wick would want the trendiest hotels." He thought for a second and then rattled off about a dozen hotel names to me. I grabbed a pen and paper out of my purse and started writing them down.

"I have a phone call to make, excuse me." Darcy exited to the kitchen.

I got the phone numbers for the hotels and started calling them one by one. First asking for Lydia, then Wick. Nothing. I was distracted watching Jane repeatedly try to call Lydia. When the fourth hotel operator said, "One moment, please," and then the line started to ring, it took me a second to realize what was happening.

"Darcy!"

Darcy came running out of the kitchen right when Wick picked up the phone.

"This better be about why our room service is taking so long," Wick slurred on the other end of my phone, loud enough for all of us to hear it.

Darcy grabbed the receiver. "I'm just calling to confirm the room number, sir," he said in an unrecognizable voice.

"What? Didn't you just call the room? How can you call a room and not know the room number? Didn't you have to dial room four two seven?"

Darcy quickly hung up. "I don't think you guys should come," he told us. "I can handle this on my own."

Of course, Jane and I ignored him and followed him out the door. Darcy didn't protest, he just sat in the front of the taxi and was on his cell phone the entire time.

Jane was practically shaking. "I can't believe how irresponsible Lydia is. They are clearly drunk, and she has the nerve to use her credit card to get an expensive hotel room to do who knows what. I'm the worst sister on earth!"

"Jane, how is any of this your fault? Lydia should know better."

She leaned back in the seat and put her hands over her face. "And here I thought everything was going to be okay, now that I was with Charles. Of course I couldn't be that lucky." I'm sure it didn't help that Charles was away with his family in Greece for the break.

We pulled up to the hotel and none of us waited for the bellman to open up the door. We hurried inside and a tall, muscular gentleman in all black approached Darcy.

"We can't gain access to the guest room floors without a key card. I didn't want to call security until you arrived."

"Security?" Jane was panicked.

"I'll handle this," Darcy assured us. He walked to the front counter and spoke to a manager. The guy stood guard near us, but didn't speak a word.

"Let's go." Darcy motioned us toward the elevator. He slid a room key into the elevator and pressed the button for the fourth floor.

"How did you get a key?" Jane asked.

Darcy ignored her. I could tell that he was trying to control himself. When the door opened to the fourth floor, he blocked the elevator door with his arm.

"We need to do this my way. You guys stay outside and I'll get Lydia to you. Let me handle Wick."

We approached room 427 and could hear blaring music coming from inside before we even rounded the corner. The man in black leaned against the wall next to the door and folded his arms. Darcy guided me and Jane to the other side of the door.

He tapped on the door. "Room service," he called out.

There was giggling coming from inside.

Wick's voice came from the other side of the door. "Did you forget something, because you were just here. . . ." The door swung open and Wick stopped in his tracks when he came face-to-face with Darcy. Wick's shirt was unbuttoned, his face unshaven, his hair a complete mess. His eyes were bloodshot and swollen.

Darcy pushed Wick to the side and entered the room. I instinctively followed him, even though he'd told me not to.

The room was in shambles. There was an empty champagne bottle on the coffee table and an open, nearly empty bottle of wine next to it.

"What the hell do you want, Will?" Wick stumbled as he backed into a couch.

"Lydia?" Darcy called out.

Jane ran into the room and grabbed her stomach as she took in the scene.

We heard moaning from the side of the couch. Jane ran over and found Lydia nearly passed out on the floor. It looked like she was about to be sick.

When Lydia looked up to see what the noise was about she smirked at her sister. "You're not the only one with a boyfriend." She hiccuped. "You think I'm such a child, but look at me. Fancy hotel room, hot boyfriend, champagne."

"See." Wick moved toward Lydia. "She's fine. We were just having some fun, blowing off some steam. No need to call the trust-fund police —"

It all happened so fast that I didn't even realize what was going on at first. Darcy grabbed Wick by his shirt and threw him up against the wall.

The man in black entered the room and stood at attention. I wanted him to get between the two of them. I was scared for Darcy.

"Get off me, Will." Wick tried to push Darcy off him, but he wasn't moving.

"Jane," Darcy said evenly. "Get Lydia out of here. Take her to my room."

The man in black handed Jane a key. I helped Jane pull Lydia up from the floor. Her body was limp and she smelled of alcohol. Lydia groaned and tried to push us away, but she didn't have the strength or motor skills to fight us off. "I don't want to leave. I want to party. Why do you have to ruin everything for me?"

"Shut up, Lydia!" Jane screamed at her.

Lydia, shocked from Jane raising her voice, stood up, and tried to gather herself. (Even I was a little frightened in that moment — Jane yelling was more jarring than Darcy having Wick pinned against a wall.)

"Come on." Jane pulled Lydia from the room.

I found myself frozen. I knew I should've followed Jane, but I was too scared to leave Darcy alone with Wick.

"Typical Will, coming in and ruining my fun," Wick said, a slow smile starting to spread across his lips. "You never seem to approve of my girlfriends, do you, Will? It's just like the last time you got in the way. That one loved me almost as much as this one. What can I say? I seem to have a way with the ladies."

Darcy threw Wick on the floor. He landed with a thud.

"Don't you dare ever talk about my sister that way." Darcy was shaking. "Wick, I'd like you to meet someone. This is Mr. Meryton. He's head of security for my father's firm." He motioned toward the gentleman, who had remained silent and at attention this entire time. "He's already familiar with your work."

Wick looked up with such hatred in his eyes.

Darcy continued. "He's going to be taking you to his office to go over with you what your very limited options are. He's also going to be discussing the various restraining orders that will be issued on behalf of my family, Jane's family, and Lizzie."

Wick got up from the floor so that he and Darcy were only inches from each other.

"Typical Will, hiding behind Daddy's money." Wick sneered.

Darcy leaned in closer. "No, I made the mistake of hiding last time. Now we're doing this out in public, and you're not going to have anywhere to hide. Everybody will know what kind of person you really are."

Darcy left Wick speechless as he pulled Mr. Meryton aside and started giving him instructions.

Wick, who was a complete mess, swayed back and forth. He looked over at me, perhaps realizing for the first time that I was in the room.

"Lizzie, how could you? *Will Darcy*, of all people. You even said yourself that he's a spoiled snob, right?"

I froze, horrified that Darcy had heard it, and repulsed with myself for not only thinking that of him, but saying that to Wick.

Wick approached me. "He thinks he's so much better than us."

"Don't lump me in with you."

"So you finally learned what I've been trying to tell you. These people aren't really worth anything, except what you can get from them. The funny thing, Will's sister wasn't even worth it." He chuckled slightly.

Something in me snapped. I stood there and watched this horrible person make fun of taking advantage of Darcy's sister.

He grabbed my arm. "I knew it was only a matter of time before you saw things my way. Don't stand here and pretend that you're better than me. You want in on the game, too, don't you? You know that it's not enough to play the piano. You're at Longbourn because you want to play the best pianos in the best places. That's nothing to be ashamed of. But you're fooling yourself if you think that you can get by on talent alone. You need connections. Talent and connections. You've got the talent part, but do you have it in you to get those connections, no matter the cost?"

I pushed his arm away from me.

Wick leaned in and whispered in my ear, "Don't be naive. You and I are cut from the same cloth."

"Leave her alone!" Darcy came over to intervene, but before I even realized what I was doing, my fist came in direct contact with Wick's face.

Wick fell to the floor and pain surged in my right hand.

Darcy's eyes were wide as he stood over Wick's unconscious body.

"Ow!" I held my throbbing hand. Darcy quickly ran over to the kitchen area and put some ice in a towel.

I'd never hit anybody in my entire life. I'd never even really thought about it. Certainly, I felt the urge my first few weeks at Longbourn, but I never thought I would actually do it.

Darcy took my hand in his and applied ice to the place of impact.

Mr. Meryton knelt down near Wick to check the extent of his injuries. He looked up and finally spoke. "Darcy" — he nodded toward me — "I like this one."

27.

WHILE MR. MERYTON WAITED FOR WICK TO WAKE UP, Darcy took me to his suite to see Jane and Lydia.

Jane was in the bathroom making Lydia take a shower. Darcy went into the kitchen and started to brew some coffee.

"How did you get this room?" I looked around at the gorgeous hotel suite that took up nearly the entire top floor. I sat down on one of the large plush couches in the living room area that faced the floor-length windows with a magnificent view of the Empire State Building. I was thankful to have something to distract me from the throbbing pain in my hand.

Darcy shrugged. "We needed a key to get upstairs, and this was the only room they had available. How's your hand?" He came over, unwrapped the towel, and gently examined my hand.

"That was stupid. I don't know what came over me."

"George Wickham — that's what came over you."

"Darcy, I'm so sorry."

"You don't have to keep apologizing." He took another towel and ran it under cold water. "Not that I didn't enjoy the spectacle, but you have to be careful with your hands, Lizzie." I hadn't even thought about how my little violent outburst would affect my playing. Darcy carefully wrapped the towel around my hand.

"Thank you."

He nodded.

"No, thank you for helping. I don't know what we would have done without you, truly."

He looked sad at my comment. "I guess I did hide behind my money today."

"What are you talking about?"

"The room? Mr. Meryton? I guess you were right about me after all."

I grabbed one of his hands with my good hand. He looked shocked. "What you did was thoughtful and kind. And I, I . . ." The words got caught in my throat.

The bathroom door opened and Jane emerged, escorting a bathrobed Lydia by the arm. "You are going to sleep this off, and I will try to think of how to explain this all to Mom and Dad." She dragged Lydia to the bedroom and put her to bed.

When Jane returned to us in the living room, she was clearly rattled and exhausted.

"What happened?" she asked when she saw my hand.

"Oh, nothing." I was completely embarrassed by my behavior.

"Darcy, how can you be laughing?" Jane scolded him.

I turned around and saw that Darcy was indeed laughing. "I'm sorry, Jane. I am, but . . ." He turned to me. "Do you want to tell her or shall I?"

I was horrified that my reputation was about to get worse. I couldn't tell if it would be better to be known as a bruiser than a charity case. But then maybe people would think twice about messing with me. . . .

Jane eyed us both suspiciously. I shrugged.

"It seems as if Miss Elizabeth Bennet has been hiding one of her many talents from us," Darcy said. "One that, I might add, I really wish I had known about earlier, as I would have approached things in a very different way."

"What?" Jane shook her head in confusion.

"I punched Wick," I admitted.

"She *knocked him out*," Darcy added.

Jane's eyes went wide. "You what?" Her shock wore off quickly, and before I knew it, she was grilling me on how it felt.

"Excuse me," Darcy interrupted. "As much as I would love to relish those details, I do have to go. I got the room for the night, so feel free to stay here. I'm going to take care of things with the front desk, so you don't have to explain any hotel charges to your parents. Mr. Meryton and I have some things we need to do."

Jane and I both expressed our deepest gratitude to Darcy. Then I filled Jane in on the details of what happened in the room after she'd left.

"I can't believe Darcy. If it weren't for him . . ." Jane looked pained for a moment. "I can't even begin to think about it. I also don't want to think about what I'm going to tell my parents. Something has to be done about Lydia. There is no way she can come back to Longbourn after this." She got up from the couch and went to the window. "I'm just tired. I don't want to talk about

Lydia anymore. I'll deal with her tomorrow. I'm sure she'll be passed out for a while. For now, there is something else I *would* like to talk about."

"Anything." I couldn't imagine what Jane was going through. I'd be willing to talk about whatever she wanted in order to get her mind off of today's nightmare.

"What were *you* doing with Will Darcy?" She winked at me.

I recounted the previous day to Jane. She'd known his mother was a performer of some kind, but hadn't realized she was a famous pianist.

"So . . ." Jane prodded me.

"So?" I replied. "So, Will Darcy isn't evil incarnate. I, however, am apparently a lousy judge of character. It nearly destroyed everybody close to me."

"You can't beat yourself up about Lydia. She would've found Wick eventually. Or some other version of him. She can always find trouble. *You* are the reason Darcy was here."

"I know — I was so lucky he was with me when you called."

Jane shook her head. "That wasn't what I meant. Lizzie, he didn't do all this for me. He didn't even do all of this to get back at Wick. Yes, those were probably huge factors, but I'm pretty sure he did this all because he cares about you."

I didn't want to admit that I was hoping that Darcy's feelings for me hadn't changed. But I couldn't really blame him if they had, after all the horrible things I'd said to him. The last two days had been great, but they couldn't erase the past.

My feelings for him had changed immensely. I was beginning to really care for Will Darcy.

28.

I SPENT THE REMAINDER OF MY SPRING BREAK STARING AT my cell phone. I naively thought that Darcy would call me. He sent me a few texts inquiring about my hand, but that was it. I didn't want to bother him after everything he had done to save Lydia from Wick, but I was hoping he'd want to see me again.

For the first time, I was excited about returning to Longbourn. I even accepted Jane's offer for a ride. Especially since Jane's parents were taking Lydia separately. After Jane told them about Lydia's behavior, Mr. and Mrs. Netherfield threatened to enroll Lydia in a strict Catholic boarding school in Maine, even though they were agnostic. They even drove up there during the break so she could see the nuns and uniforms and gated fence (and, most important, not a single boy in sight). I believe the term "scared straight" was coined because of places like that.

Nothing at school really changed after spring break, but I felt hopeful for once. The recital was coming up in a couple weeks, and despite not practicing as much as I wanted to because of my sore hand, I was making great progress with Rhapsody. Practice with the orchestra started the week we arrived back, and although the majority of the students in the orchestra despised me even more because I was being featured in the concert, the practices went well.

I was even excited about work, convinced that Darcy would return to his regular visits. But he didn't. I wouldn't have even known he was back on Pemberley's campus if it wasn't for Jane.

But fortunately, Jane was back with Charles, which meant that she was happy . . . and that I was able to get Darcy intel.

Jane returned from a date in a particularly good mood. "So, Charles thought it would be fun for a bunch of us to go out to dinner on Saturday."

"A bunch of us?"

"Yes. I know how much you normally dread these invitations, but for some reason, I think you might actually want to come this time. But if you don't . . ."

Jane wasn't one for teasing, but after all the grief I had given her over the course of the year about going out, I fully deserved this ribbing.

"I think I can suffer through it."

She patted me lightly on the shoulder. "Thank you for making such a sacrifice."

"That's what friends are for. Speaking of friends, do you know which of Charles's friends are going to be there?" I tried to look innocent.

"Let's see, I don't know. Charles has so many friends. . . ."

She wasn't going to let me get away with this so easily.

"Fine. Is Will Darcy going to be there?"

"Darcy . . . Darcy . . ." Jane tapped her lips and she rolled the name around on her tongue. "The name is familiar. Yes, Darcy . . . I believe he is going to be there."

"Thank you. I *guess* I could make an appearance. I don't want to be rude."

She laughed. "No, we wouldn't want that. Plus, it will be so much fun!"

How many times had Jane said that to me? How many times had I scoffed at her bright disposition?

But for the first time, I sincerely believed that I would have fun.

We were among the first people to arrive at the restaurant. Jane sat next to Charles at the head of the table, and I sat next to her. I put my purse on the chair next to mine, reserving it for Darcy. A few other students started shuffling in, including Colin and Charlotte, who sat directly across from me. There were only two seats left open, the one next to me and another seat on the opposite side of the table, farthest away from me.

Darcy walked in and apologized for being late. I smiled at him and he briefly glanced in my direction. I took my purse off the chair and put it on the floor next to me. He walked around the entire table and sat in the other seat.

Charles announced that one of his friends just texted that he couldn't make it so we were all there.

My spirits sank as I realized that my evening would be spent with Jane and Charles in deep conversation to my left and Colin and Charlotte in front of me straining to talk about anything. And to my right, an empty seat.

I kept leaning over to hear what Darcy was talking about at the other side of the table, trying to find a way to join his conversation. But it was hopeless; there were four people between us, and I didn't really know any of them well. I tried to catch his glance so I could smile at him to show that I was a friendly person, not the horrific person who'd berated him for asking me to prom.

But Darcy just stared ahead or would politely nod in response to something someone said to him. I was desperate for confirmation that our friendly encounters over spring break hadn't been a fluke.

"So," Charles said loudly, commanding the attention of the group, "it's good to be back. Greece was wonderful, but I missed being with friends." He winked at Jane. "What did everybody do on their break?"

Charles had Charlotte start, and slowly everybody went around the table talking about vacations, beach houses, Europe, and, of course, prom-dress fittings. I waited patiently for Darcy's turn to come, to see if he would mention me.

But when it came time for Darcy to talk, he shrugged. "Nothing special, just spent time with my family." He looked to the person across the table from him, signaling that he wouldn't be elaborating further.

So I did receive confirmation, but not the kind that I wanted. It was clear that I was no longer of interest to Will Darcy.

"Lizzie?" Charles called to me. I was in such a daze that I hadn't realized it was my turn.

"Oh, I had a good break, thanks." I looked toward Darcy. "I had some friends come and visit me and that was fun. I, uh, went to this amazing concert at Carnegie Hall. . . ."

"What? No prom shopping?" the guy next to Darcy asked.

"No, I'm not going to prom."

One would think that after that embarrassing admission (at least in this company) there would be an awkward pause around the table. But at the mere mention of the word *prom*, discussions started going around the table about dinner reservations and after-party plans. Maybe they didn't want to acknowledge that I wasn't going.

Despite the fact that I was surrounded by more than a dozen people in a crowded restaurant, a feeling of loneliness swept over me. It certainly wasn't the first time I'd felt alone on campus. But this was worse. Because not only did I feel alone, but there was a reminder on the other side of the table of what I could've had. At that point, it might as well have been the other side of the world, but there *was* someone I wanted to be with.

29.

AFTER THE DINNER, JANE OFFERED TO TALK TO CHARLES TO see if he could give any insight to Darcy's behavior, but I felt it was useless. There was only one thing that I had control over at that point — my performance in the following week's recital.

I threw myself into practice, running through my piece over and over every day. I felt more pressure when I noticed that the posters for the spring recital featured my name: "Performance of Rachmaninoff's Rhapsody on a Theme of Paganini by Elizabeth Bennet and the Longbourn Orchestra."

During class I would stare at my desk and pretend it was a keyboard, going over the piece in my head.

I was at Longbourn to get an education, to get better at music. Prom, boys, anything else was just a distraction to me at that point. I ignored all the girls talking about the dance, which was the weekend after the recital. I would zip past them as they held fashion shows in the hallway. I didn't even glance at their designer dresses.

I had never been so focused on a performance in my life. I found myself getting annoyed when the orchestra couldn't keep up or someone missed her cue. Part of me was convinced they were doing it on purpose, that there was a desire among the students to see me fall flat on my face. But I was going to do everything in my power to nail my part. They could screw up, but once I started playing, there wasn't anything they could really do to stop me.

The evening of the performance came. I briefly saw my parents for a late lunch, but I could hardly eat. My nerves were getting the best of me.

The Longbourn auditorium was an old building, with stained-glass windows and a large balcony. All of our performances for music and drama were held in this space and it seated nearly five hundred people. It was tradition for parents to come up for the recital and there was always a lavish reception afterward.

I sat by myself backstage in a practice room with my head-phones on, listening to Rhapsody. Our performance was the finale for the evening, and I didn't want to get distracted by lis-tening to the various performances by members of the orchestra and the other piano students.

My legs began to twitch. I closed my eyes and tried some breath-ing exercises to calm down. I nearly screamed out when someone tapped me on the shoulder to notify me that it was time.

We were all dressed in floor-length black dresses. I had my hair tied back in a loose bun that Jane had done for me.

I waited in the wings as the members of the orchestra took their places to the applause of the audience. Mrs. Gardiner then took center stage and motioned for me to make my entrance.

I tried to walk out with confidence, but felt my nerves increase with each step. I looked up toward the lights as I took my bow. The lights temporarily blinded me so I couldn't see the audi-ence. The white light that was burned into my gaze gave me something to concentrate on as I sat down at the piano.

I gently guided my hands up and down the keyboard. Mrs. Gardiner was waiting for my signal to start, and I needed this quick moment to re-familiarize myself with the keys. I'd been playing piano for more than a decade, but this little ritual was something I did before every performance. I wanted to, in some way, connect with the instrument before I played.

I looked at Mrs. Gardiner and nodded. She held up her baton and the entire orchestra flipped their instruments to attention. At that very moment, I was nearly bursting with a desire to start. The nerves subsided and this gush of energy rushed forth as I eagerly anticipated the motion of the baton that would start the piece.

Mrs. Gardiner flicked the baton down. The strings started to play and I answered with chords. The beginning was the easiest (if anything by Rachmaninoff could be considered easy) and soon I found myself in a wonderful zone where I let my fingers do what I'd practiced them to do. They happily slid across the piano as I gave myself over to the music.

This was when I truly felt alive. No matter if I was answering the orchestra with runs or large bundles of notes or quietly building anticipation for the next variation, there was nowhere else I wanted to be but at Longbourn, on that stage, with this orchestra.

Nearly fifteen minutes into the piece, as I started in by myself on the eighteenth variation, the audience began to applaud. This section was my favorite, not just because it was featured in many romantic movies, but it was beautiful. When the orchestra joined in with me, I felt a lump in my throat.

As we finished that section, I took a deep breath. I needed every ounce of energy and concentration to get through the end.

As I began to tackle Rachmaninoff's challenging runs, a trickle of sweat began to make its way down the side of my face. I might not have even breathed for the last minute or so while I hammered away at the keyboard. Every note rang out and I leaned forward into the keys. It was a race to the finish, and after one last run and the crescendo of the orchestra, all fell silent as I played the last two chords.

I dropped my hands into my lap from exhaustion. The audience erupted in applause. I looked at Mrs. Gardiner and she motioned for me to stand up. As I did, she enveloped me in a huge hug. "Thank you, Elizabeth," she whispered in my ear. "That was wonderful!"

I nodded and went to shake the hands of the two first-chair violinists, Mary and Kitty, which was customary when playing with an orchestra.

I finally faced the audience and noticed they were on their feet. I bowed and motioned toward the orchestra, who then stood up.

For the first time, I surveyed the audience. I did notice that not everybody was standing; several students from my classes sat looking completely bored, but their parents seemed impressed.

And then in the third row, I saw my parents, both with tears streaming down their faces. I nearly started to sob, but the sight of Darcy, Georgiana, and their mom standing next to my parents shocked the tears from my system.

30.

THE RECEPTION WAS HELD IN FOUNDERS HALL, THE SAME place the mixer had been at the beginning of the semester. It was beautifully decorated with flowers and candles. I was having difficulty finding my parents; anytime I tried to locate them, someone would come up and congratulate me. Granted, the majority of people coming up to me were adults; even an inspiring performance of Rachmaninoff wasn't going to erase the scholarship stamp across my face.

After profusely thanking the headmistress for her kind words,

I made a beeline for the food, as I knew that was where my dad would most likely be.

"There you are!" he exclaimed while holding a plate full of crudités.

Mom came rushing over and hugged me tightly. "Oh, Lizzie!" I felt my chin twitch as she held on to me. "You were wonderful. Your father and I are so proud of you."

Dad leaned over and planted a kiss on my forehead. "Amazing. I have no idea where you get any of your talent. It certainly isn't from either of us."

Mom hit him. "You promised you wouldn't embarrass her."

My parents were always overly sensitive about their behavior at Longbourn. They'd never monitored themselves when I had been at school back home, and they certainly didn't care about embarrassing me in front of my Hoboken friends, but I think the Longbourn parents made them even more uncomfortable than they made me.

"Lizzie!" Georgie ran up to me with a dozen red roses. "These are for you. From *all of us*."

"Thank you!" I smelled the flowers. "You shouldn't have."

"Nonsense." Claudia Reynolds came up to me and grabbed my hands. "It is customary for the soloist to be given roses. Especially after that performance. You were brilliant, my dear."

"Thank you. You have no idea how much that means coming from you." I still couldn't believe that Claudia Reynolds even knew who I was, but at that moment, there was only one person's review that I wanted to hear.

I turned hopefully to Darcy.

He came over and kissed me on the cheek. "Amazing."

"Thanks. I can't believe you guys came."

"Of course we would be here. We weren't going to miss it for anything." He smiled at me, and for a moment I sensed that Spring Break Darcy was back.

For the second time that evening, a sense of urgency overtook me. But this time it wasn't to perform, it was to come clean. I grabbed Darcy by the arm and started to lead him out of the room.

"Can I talk to you?" I asked.

"Uh, of course." He seemed surprised by my forwardness, but not nearly as shocked as I was.

We arrived outside Founders Hall, and he stood there with a puzzled look on his face.

"So . . ." I tried to figure out what I wanted to say to him. For weeks I had wanted nothing more than to talk to him, but I figured that he would do the talking. I realized that for most of the time I knew him, he instigated our conversations. It had been my job to rudely reply back to him.

"I'm sorry, Darcy. I'm really sorry."

Darcy looked at me. "I keep telling you, there is nothing you have to apologize for."

"Yes I do. I'm sorry that I said all those horrible things about you to Wick, that I thought you were this stuck-up snob." His jaw clenched at hearing those words. "But the thing is, you weren't the snob. I was. You were right — I did have a problem with people with money. I built this wall up around me — I didn't want to get hurt. When I first met you, you seemed like every other person at Pemberley, and I refused, despite your efforts to get to know me better, to change my stubborn mind.

"Maybe we do have a lot more in common than I thought. You didn't want to trust any scholarship students. And I really don't blame you after what Wick did, and knowing how that affected you. . . . Even after that, you still could see past my circumstances and see *me*. I'm so horrified by my behavior. You tried to be nice to me and I just dismissed you. You didn't have to do any of those things — giving me the coat and the tickets to see your mom, introducing me to your family, and helping with Lydia. In fact, I wouldn't blame you if you never wanted to speak to me again. But, the thing is, I'm ready to take down the wall, and I really hope that we can be . . ."

I suddenly didn't know what to say next. I couldn't say *friends*, as I knew deep down that wasn't what I wanted from Darcy.

Darcy folded his arms. "Lizzie, does this have anything to do with the fact that prom is next weekend?"

"Prom? No, not at all."

He nodded slowly. "Good, because there is something you should know. I have no intention of asking you to prom."

31.

ARCY'S WORDS HUNG IN THE AIR FOR WHAT SEEMED LIKE an eternity. Truth be told, there were only a couple seconds between that statement and what followed, but to me those two seconds were painful.

A person can think a lot of things in two seconds: how foolish she's been, how awful a person she's been, that maybe she's no better than Caroline Bingley, that maybe Longbourn has changed her for the worse.

I tried desperately to hide any emotion from Darcy. He had

every reason not to want to go to prom with me. And I didn't really care about prom anyway.

I cared about Darcy.

Although he already made it clear to me that he had no intention of making the same mistake twice. *I* was that mistake.

At least, in those two seconds, I thought I was.

"Lizzie," he said, tucking a stray lock of hair behind my ear. "Prom is a stupid, inconsequential event. In the past few weeks, I've seen friends ask girls to prom who they don't even like. Why? So they can have a date. It's a silly tradition that I have no desire to take you to."

I nodded at him. Trying, for the second time this evening, to fight back tears. But these were a different kind of tears than earlier. My heart was starting to tear in two.

Darcy picked up my hand. "You are far too important and special to me to take to such an uninspiring event."

I looked up at him. He smiled at me and bent down on one knee. "Elizabeth Bennet, will you do me the great honor of *not* going to prom with me?"

I stared blankly at him for a few seconds. Then I took him in, kneeling before me, giving me the best proposal of all. I couldn't help but laugh at his wonderful gesture. "Yes, I will."

"Will you instead avoid prom with me and let me take you on a date?"

"Yes."

He stood up and put his arms around me. "You have no idea how much agony I have been in these last few weeks."

I pulled away. "Why?"

Darcy sighed. "You seem to forget who my mother is. I knew better than to even approach you with anything while you were getting ready for the concert. Especially knowing that you have a pretty ferocious right hook."

The realization that Darcy wasn't ignoring me because of any ill feelings was a huge relief.

"And your absence from the Junction?"

He bit his lower lip and curled his arm around my waist. "I'm sorry to inform you that I have your shifts on my calendar and I'll see you tomorrow night."

"Thanks for the warning." I placed my head against his chest.

"Oh, and one more thing I should warn you about." I was so comfortable; I nuzzled my head into his shoulder for him to continue. "I'm going to take you to a very casual, very non-Pemberley place for our date. There will be no crystal, no foie anything, and, more important, no crazy prom parties. Just you, me, and some delicious Italian food."

"Sounds perfect."

32.

PROM NIGHT ARRIVED. JANE SPENT MOST OF THE DAY GETTING a spray tan, manicure, pedicure, and her hair done.

"Are you sure you don't want to borrow anything for tonight?" she offered.

I looked down at my generic jeans and V-necked top and shook my head. "No, I'm good."

I helped Jane with her dress, a beautiful, red strapless gown. We went into the common room and I volunteered to take pictures for everybody before the media arrived. Charlotte was equally gorgeous in her cream, beaded spaghetti-strap floor-length gown.

Everybody looked stunning (even Caroline, who was going with a guy from the city). Every hair was sprayed into place, every nail filed to perfection, everything done to the standard of a proper Longbourn lady.

I wished them all a good evening and headed down the long staircase. Below me were dozens of Pemberley guys decked out in tuxes, corsages in hand. I'm sure my common appearance was the last thing they were expecting to see, but they weren't who I was looking for.

Darcy stepped forward among the crowd — he stuck out like a sore thumb with his jeans, T-shirt, and sneakers. He bowed down to greet me and we both laughed.

He held my hand as we got into a taxi. As we drove away, I thought about all the girls who were going to prom tonight. They may have been happy with their fake eyelashes and hair extensions. But that wasn't what I wanted.

What Darcy and I had was better than any prom or custom couture dress.

Because what we had was real.

Acknowledgments

EVEN THOUGH MY NAME APPEARS ON THE COVER, THERE ARE so many people responsible for this book in your hands.

I'm so lucky to have one of the best editors in the business, David Levithan. Thank you for your constant support of my writing. I don't know how you do all that you do. You are truly an inspiration, my friend. Although I'm still not entirely convinced that you are human.

Jodi Reamer, my fearless agent, was in my corner years before I was even published. Thank you for staying with me and still talking to me even after reading all those awful drafts.

Bushels of gratitude to everybody at Scholastic, especially: Erin Black for revisiting Miss Austen with me, Elizabeth B. Parisi for a fabulous cover design, Susan Jeffers Casel for your copyediting brilliance, Sheila Marie Everett for not taking it personally when I bust out laughing when I introduce her as my publicist, Leslie Garych, Tracy van Straaten, Julie Amitie, Emily Sharpe, and all of the sales reps for their constant enthusiasm.

I bow down to Bethany Strout and Jennifer Leonard for once again giving me such thoughtful reader's comments. I really appreciate you both taking the time to help me with this story. I can pretty much guarantee that I'll be bugging you both again. This is what you get for being so good!

I would be lost without Kirk Benshoff (Violet's Dad) and his amazing website design and tech expertise. Seriously, I'd be curled up under my desk if it weren't for you! I'm also lucky to have a great friend and blog proofreader in Natalie Thrasher.

I'm grateful to have such a wonderful support system of friends and family who understand when Author Elizabeth goes into hiding to write. I'd especially like to thank Stephenie Meyer for being so enthusiastic for my writer life and having that conversation about *Pride and Prejudice* that led me to the idea for this book.

To all the booksellers, librarians, and bloggers who have supported me as an author — I know how many books are out there and I'm truly honored when anybody picks mine up. Thank you for giving me a chance.

And of course there's Jane, the lovely Miss Austen. No one could ever touch what you have created. *Prom and Prejudice* is simply my attempt to pay homage to your brilliant work and to celebrate you as what you will forever be known as — one of the greatest authors of all time.